PRA...
BEATRI...

LEFT ON A DOORSTEP
The DuPree Dynasty – Book One

"Beatrice Crew's novel Left on a Doorstep is a compelling nineteenth-century, late Victorian era romance and mystery. The characters are well-developed and dialogue is used effectively to carry the story along. The engaging descriptive narrative is well-orchestrated, giving the reader a solid sense of time and place. The author knows the late Victorian era well and this is evident in her storytelling talents. There is a building tension as the mystery thickens and the romance evolves, making for an enormously enjoyable read."

—Emily-Jane Hills Orford for *Readers' Favorite*

"Left on a Doorstep by Beatrice H. Crew is a beautiful historical tale of love, deceit, greed, kindness, and sacrifice. The plot had a unique depth. I loved the realistic storyline which still applies to the current world: the eternal message that people can often be cold and evil! Beatrice is a gifted storyteller, who pulled at my heartstrings with this emotional read. Her writing was stylish, and the story was easy to follow. . . . Thumbs up to Beatrice on this beautiful book. I look forward to more in the future."

—Jennifer Ibiam for *Readers' Favorite*

"Beatrice H. Crew has written a highly captivating novel set in nineteenth-century London. Left on a Doorstep is a must-read for everyone who enjoys a historical romance story. Crew does an exceptional job of keeping the reader glued to the book: it wasn't easy to put down. Bravo, Beatrice H. Crew. You have written a novel that readers will enjoy for years to come. I look forward to your future work."

—Teresa Syms for *Readers' Favorite*

"Left on a Doorstep by Beatrice H. Crew was like watching those romantic movies set in the 1800s, or . . . Bridgerton. . . . A delightful read . . . . From its catchy title to the historically appropriate settings, clothing, pastimes, foods, mannerisms, terms of endearment, characters, and dialogue, this novel will please ardent historical romance fans. It is a well-executed blend of mystery and romance that can even win over non-romance readers like me. I thoroughly enjoyed it!"

—Viga Boland for *Readers' Favorite*

"Beatrice H. Crew spins a web of suspense that blends murder, mystery, and family issues into one unpredictable piece of entertainment. . . . I enjoyed the storyline and found the ending a surprise. The author reveals little acts of kindness can make just as large a wave of events as leaving a child on a doorstep for her safety."

—Peggy Jo Wipf for *Readers' Favorite*

Left on a Doorstep

The DuPree Dynasty
Book One

By

Beatrice H. Crew

See Beyond the Sea

During the day, you put on a mask to show your bravery
Because many aspects of your life seem unsavory.

You feel the need to hide your true face
By keeping your mask firmly in place.

You must decide which path to take
And hope you don't make a mistake.

Remember the baby bird that depends on its parents from birth
Must one day step from the nest to soar above the earth.

But if you can find a way to overcome and break free,
You will safely sail like a ship on the North Sea.

As the sun over the sea sinks below the horizon,
Know that tomorrow, once again, it will start rising.

Even though it's hard to do, reach up and pull the mask away.
You will be able to see the start of a brand-new day.

Beatrice H. Crew
July 24, 2021

Acknowledgments

Milan Sergent, you are my entire world!
Your support and guidance mean more than you will ever know. From reading drafts, giving advice, and helping design a beautiful cover, you have been there for me. Your love brings light to each day and a feeling of safety each night. Writing a romance novel isn't difficult with you as the best example of love.

Thank you to Melinda Guillemette, Pat Ladnier, Mary Ann Graham, Stacey Wane, and Janet Scott. Your insight was invaluable.

Diane Anderson, your contribution to this book gave life to one of my characters. Her original name didn't feel right, so I asked for suggestions. Your submission (Emma) was the perfect one! Thank you.

Table of Contents

Prologue

North Sea
DuPree Island
November 1875

John and Rebecca DuPree were grateful they had a few minutes to enjoy the October winter weather, which was unusually mild for England's eastern coastline. As they walked along the edge of the water, the crunch of sand under their feet, the gentle crash of waves against the shoreline, and the call of seagulls were the only sounds filling the air.

Idle chatter wasn't necessary. Their joy of being together was so great they did not need to speak. Having this time alone refreshed their souls. Sleepless nights with a teething baby had taken a toll on their nerves.

"Darling, I simply adore Victoria so much, but I appreciate getting a break," Rebecca spoke quietly, before standing on tiptoes to kiss his cheek. "She is growing so fast."

"Sweetheart, I know it's exhausting with her teething, but soon she'll be back on her normal schedule," John assured her.

"What was that sound?" Rebecca's eyes frantically searched the beach.

"I didn't hear anything. What do you think it was?" John glanced around cautiously, trying to spot any danger. As he turned back to Rebecca, she crumpled to her knees in the wet sand and almost toppled over. One hand clutched her heart while the other pointed to the tall cliffs ahead. Not a word escaped from her gaping mouth.

Suddenly, the wind brought the faint sound of a baby's cry to his ears. With a racing pulse, John swiveled to see what Rebecca was pointing at.

He thought his heart would stop.

Oh, God! Not again, John's mind screamed.

Could he reach them in time?

Leaving his wife, Rebecca, behind on the beach, he ran full speed toward the obscured pathway he knew was ahead. The gravel trail would lead him behind where his mother stood at the edge of the highest point on the island. She faced the side of the sea without a beach and where the waves raged in a fury. A strong wind blew her hair and skirts around her wildly. Twice John almost lost his footing as he ascended the rocky cliffside but was able to quickly recover.

He reached the top and blinked, hoping to clear his vision and confirm what he saw was not real. Instead, hearing his baby girl's cries proved what he saw was happening.

His mother held a squirming Victoria high over her head; she was preparing to fling the baby into the sea.

Chapter One: No Good Deed

London, England
Montgomery Townhouse
March 1896

SALLY, we have to keep moving. Your father isn't far behind," Victoria said, urging the fourteen-year-old down the back street of one of the seedy parts of London as the girl clutched her belly.

"Miss Victoria, the pain be gettin' real bad. The babe be comin'." Sally couldn't run, and every time a sharp pain hit, she would have to stop and double over until it passed.

Looking back, Victoria saw two men following them. They were a couple of blocks away. Whitehaven, the home for unwed mothers, was up ahead. Could they reach the safety of the massive wooden doors before the men caught them?

As they reached the stone steps leading to Whitehaven, a

shot of pain caused Sally to fall to the ground. Victoria tried to urge her to stand, but Sally couldn't move until the pain was over. Should Victoria run up the steps to get help? Should she shout for somebody in such a dangerous area?

Before she could do anything, a rough hand clasped over her mouth. Hot beer breath laced with garlic blew against her neck and almost caused her to throw up in her mouth. The smell of sweat added to her nausea. Sally's father pulled her back with such force, nearly knocking her feet out from under her.

"You'll die t'night. You whore! You want to steal me girl?"

The sharp blade of a knife digging into the flesh of her throat caused Victoria to screech at the pain.

Victoria awoke with a jolt. Twice over the last week, while asleep, her mind had exaggerated the details of an incident where she had helped a young pregnant girl escape her abusive father. At least she didn't scream and disturb the household this time.

She had never been involved in the rescue of an unwed mother before. However, she was the fundraising chair for the board of directors of The Whitehaven Rescue Home and Hospital for Unmarried Mothers. Poor living conditions meant many unwed women passed away in childbirth, and their children ended up in orphanages. Whitehaven was one of the organizations created in London that helped these women with shelter, food, clothing, medical care, and education.

As the fundraising chair, Victoria attended ladies'

2

luncheons and conferences and invited affluent women to teas at her family's townhouse to solicit funds for unfortunate women and their children.

Earlier in the week, Victoria attended a board meeting in the conference room of Whitehaven, where the board discussed the work they needed to do. More volunteers and money were at the top of the agenda.

Victoria was so focused on writing down notes and the ideas discussed during the meeting; she didn't realize she was the last board member remaining in the conference room. She asked the butler to have her carriage brought round so she could go home.

Victoria stepped out on the stoop to wait. She noticed a young girl, exceptionally large with child, standing across the street. The girl was visibly shaking, and tears were glistening on her cheeks.

Compassion gripped Victoria's heart, and she crossed the street to see if she could help.

"Hello, my name is Victoria. What's your name?" Victoria tried to appear calm, but she had never spoken to anyone from that part of London. The girl was relatively clean and smelled of lye soap.

"Miss, my name is Sally. Oh!" she groaned and clutched her belly.

"Sally, you need to sit down. Let me help you to a bench. I see a secluded one behind this tree." Victoria took Sally's arm and helped her slowly move to the bench and carefully sit down.

"Sally, can I go find someone from Whitehaven and get you safely inside?"

"No! Miss Victoria, if me dad finds out I'm even talkin' to you, he'll beat me."

"Why would he beat you?"

Sally turned ashen, and her chest panted.

"Look, I know you are in some kind of trouble. I can help you if only you tell me what it is," said Victoria, trying to sound friendly.

"Me mum died when I were five. I had to cook and clean for me dad. When I turned twelve, me dad made me lie with his friends for money. I close me eyes and try not to think till it be over." Sally gasped and sniffled. "Now that I am with babe, he said he'll sell it. He brags he'll be rich. Miss, I have to get home 'fore me dad does. His friend Joe will be coming to lie with me tonight. Me dad said that would make me babe come tomorrow. I'm afeared Joe will hurt me babe. His shaft is the biggest of all I lie with," Sally said, with such a look of terror, it reached out and touched Victoria's very soul.

Victoria couldn't catch her breath. Who would do such a thing to their own flesh and blood?

"Sally, you came here today because you want a better life for you and your baby. Let me help you find a way to escape. We need to make a plan. When will your father get home? Will he leave later? You need to be gone before Joe gets there."

"Me dad will be home at five then leave around ten to go to the pub. Me dad said Joe is coming over around eleven," Sally said, still shaking from fear. She bit her bottom lip and moaned with pain.

"Then you need to leave after your dad does. Give

4

him ten minutes to get to the pub, then sneak out. Where can you meet me?"

"The best place is on the outskirts of White Chapel . . . ."

With a quivering hand, Victoria wrote down the address to give to the hackney driver.

"Miss, you be kind, but you be in danger if me dad learns of it," Sally sighed, but Victoria could see a glimmer of hope in her eyes.

"I will borrow a servant's uniform, hire a hackney, meet you, and bring you to Whitehaven. Trust me. Your dad won't be able to get to you if you seek help there. They will keep you safe." Victoria tried to sound brave, but she was frightened down to the soles of her shoes.

"Miss, I will meet you after ten. If you don't come, I won't blame you. I know you've never been to the slums, and I don't want you to get hurt."

"Sally, I will be there. I promise." Victoria gave her hands a quick squeeze.

A few minutes after nine o'clock, Victoria changed, and secretly left her parents' townhouse through the back gate of the enclosed garden. A servant found her a hackney. She traveled to one of the most notorious slum areas in East London. Sally promised to meet Victoria on the outskirts of White Chapel. Unfortunately, many roads were unmade and difficult for carriages to navigate without getting bogged in the mud and the almost total lack of drainage. The smell of human waste, mixed with horse dung, rotting garbage, mold, and mildew, was so overpowering Victoria almost threw up. She found it was better when she breathed through her mouth. She had never seen such rats as the ones in this section of London. They were as large as house cats.

Victoria had led a sheltered life and had only heard of the squalor the poor of London faced each day. But, seeing the ill-lit streets, overcrowding, unsanitary, and squalid living conditions made her realize she should do more than just sit on a board of directors.

As promised, Sally was waiting for her in the shadow of a crumbling tenant building. Seeing Victoria, the poor girl hobbled as fast as possible in her condition toward the hackney. The driver offered to help, but Sally pulled herself in with only Victoria's help. Both were scared and shaking as they traveled to Whitehaven. Not until the big heavy doors closed behind them did either say a word.

"Miss Victoria, I can't believe the plan worked. I was so afraid me dad wouldn't leave. He kept patting me belly and talking about the money he would make from sellin' the babe t'morrow." Sally cried as she thanked Victoria over and over.

Whitehaven's matron sent a message to Victoria the next afternoon announcing that Sally had given birth. As soon as Sally could move, they would transfer her to another home twenty miles away to guarantee that her father wouldn't be able to find her.

"Mother, helping Sally escape her evil father was the scariest thing I have ever done but also the most rewarding. I know I should have discussed it with you and Father, but I knew time was of the essence," Victoria said, one afternoon during tea.

"When you told us what you did, I thought my heart would stop. I am proud of you but also can't believe you were so reckless. What if Sally's father had hurt you? I try to not think of what could have happened.

"To know there are men in this world who will sell their daughters' babies for money is atrocious. Didn't you say Sally's father was going to sell the baby to a rich couple who couldn't have children of their own?" Mother asked, squeezing her eyes shut.

"Sally told me that was his plan. I know it must be hard for couples who want children to find they cannot. But to buy a baby illegally is more than I can imagine. Do they turn a blind eye?" Victoria's expression hardened at the thought.

"I was terrified rescuing Sally," said Victoria, with much conviction, "but I am so glad she and her baby are safe.

"Mother, you have always been involved with helping unfortunate women, and you encouraged me to be on the board of Whitehaven. I have been thinking, and I want to do more than just sit on a board. I want to help other young unwed mothers have better lives. One or two girls drown themselves in the nearby river at our country estate and the surrounding area every year. I did not realize the

7

reason was that they were with child and not married. They didn't want to bring shame to their families and believed that drowning was their only recourse."

She and her mother discussed ways to provide resources to anyone needing help and implement them when they returned to their country estate in a couple of months.

Two weeks later, Emma Jonas, her companion, rushed into her room.

"Oh, Victoria! One of the chambermaids told me Sally's father found out you were the one who stole his daughter from him. He has sworn to find you and make you pay," she said, twisting her hands. "From what I have been told, he has many unsavory friends who will help him in his quest."

"This is distressing news. I will let my parents know at once. Thank you, Emma," Victoria said, with a quiver in her voice.

Her parents decided to remove to the country estate earlier than usual. The household at once started packing, and within two days, they were on the road.

Would Victoria be safe? If Sally's dad wanted to find her, she would be in danger even in the country. She didn't know what he looked like nor his name. He could be anywhere.

Chapter Two:
Mission Impossible

WALKING down the hall to Lord John's suite of rooms, Allistair thought about how he appreciated growing up on DuPree Island. Any young boy would enjoy exploring, learning, and playing there. His father, Paul, had been a hardworking man but always made time for him. He taught Allistair to fish, and most of all, passed on his love for horses. From the time Allistair could walk, he was at his father's side as he raised, trained, and cared for the animals.

When he turned six, Allistair's father died from an accident, trying to fix one of the wheat-harvesting machines.

"Thank goodness the boy's father died quickly and did not suffer. With his injury, he could have lingered for days or weeks without a chance of making a full recovery," said the farm manager, when he didn't know Allistair was within hearing distance.

Allistair was glad his father had not suffered, but he and his mother had.

Now Lord John had terminal cancer, and the doctor had only given him a couple of years at the most to live. Lord John tried to hide how ill he felt, but Allistair was relieved that he had finally asked for medical assistance.

Sitting at Lord John's bedside, Allistair hoped that this man, he considered his second father, would rally. To see him in the bed was unsettling, but he was the strongest human Allistair knew, and with all the adversity he had faced and overcome, indeed, he had a great chance of living much longer.

Even with all that life had thrown Lord John's way, he had remained upbeat and kept a great outlook, Allistair thought. As a young boy, Lord John lost his baby sister, Karen, when his mother threw her into the sea. Then after finding true love with his wife, Rebecca, Lord John's mother tried to throw his baby girl, Victoria, into the sea as well.

That was not the end of tragedies to befall Lord John. Months later, that same baby died on a return trip from the mainland and had her burial at sea. Two years later, he was excited about the birth of another child, but tragedy struck yet again; Rebecca died in childbirth. A weaker man would have fallen under such heartache, but Lord John knew he had the responsibility of raising his son, Daniel, and keeping the island operations productive. The islanders were counting on him.

"Allistair, my son," Lord John said with a raspy voice,

unlike his usual deep, strong tone. "I regret your father isn't here to see the man you have become. Caught up in my grief, I didn't realize your mother had lost her way, and you were an afterthought. She had to take time to work through her sorrow. In the meanwhile, you ran wild over the island with no sense of direction. When I saw you going the wrong way, I stepped in and moved you to the manor. I taught you all about running the estate and noticed your true passion was for the horses.

"You became a big brother to Daniel and helped me raise him as I know Rebecca would have wanted. You are my son, too. You and Daniel will run the many operations here on the island when I am no longer here with you.

"That will be many years from now." It pained Allistair to hear him talk about dying.

"I'm afraid not. That's why I have two missions for you. First, I need you to write to Daniel, asking him to come home from university. I do not want to alarm Daniel, so tell him we have a surprise for him. Since the school term has ended, he will not miss any classes. I know he planned to travel the continent with his friends but tell him this surprise is worth giving up the trip."

"I will send Daniel a note right away," said Allistair. "Telling him it's a surprise will bring him home faster."

"Allistair, the second mission is harder. I have a secret to tell you that will surprise you. I am sorry I could not tell you before now. Please do not judge me harshly. Rebecca and I knew we had to keep this from everyone." Lord John looked at him with tears in his eyes.

"I could never think harshly of you."

11

Allistair knew that Lord John had a good reason for keeping his secret and was honored that he trusted him.

Lord John stopped to drink a few sips of water.

"I can come back in a couple of hours if you need to rest," Allistair mentioned, after seeing Lord John's fatigue.

"I need to reveal my secret to you and ask you to take care of an important mission for me. You were a young boy of five when we lost your father and my daughter, Victoria. I am not sure how much you remember about Victoria since you were grieving your father, but she was the apple of my eye."

"I could not imagine everything you went through since I don't have children of my own yet," said Allistair. "I remember playing with her when she was learning to crawl. Seeing her rock back and forth, trying to create the momentum needed to crawl, was so cute. I would sit on the floor across the room and call to her. With a small laugh, she would crawl as fast as she could to get to me. I am so sorry she passed away."

Lord John nodded. "I thought I would die when I saw my mother holding Victoria high overhead, ready to throw her into the sea. Rebecca refused to let her out of her sight even after we moved Esther to the tower with a full-time companion to watch her. Rebecca did not get any rest unless I was with baby Victoria. I thought she would get sick from her worry.

"Allistair, no one knows what I am about to tell you. Rebecca and I devised a plan to keep Victoria safe. We informed everyone that we were taking the baby to meet Rebecca's side of the family. But that was not the truth.

12

We didn't trust that Esther wouldn't find a way to harm Victoria."

Allistair sat up with a start, holding his breath, waiting for Lord John to tell him more.

"In London, Rebecca's oldest brother had a best friend who couldn't have a child. Our plan was to leave Victoria on their doorstep, where we knew the friend would find her. All these years, she has lived as their daughter and does not know about the adoption."

Lord John gave Allistair a pleading look. "I need you to bring her home. Will you do that for me?"

"Lord John, I am shaken, to say the least, but I know you did what you thought was best for Victoria. Yes, I will complete both missions for you, but I'm going to leave you now. I can see how exhausted you are, so I'll come back later this afternoon," Allistair said, returning the chair to its original location.

"Please don't tell anyone we've talked about this. Until Victoria agrees to come, I don't want to upset the family with the revelation that she is still alive."

Agreeing with Lord John, Allistair quickly exited the room and went to the beach. He knew he needed to think about everything.

Allistair took out one of the rowboats and worked up a sweat, traveling around to the other side of the island, where the water moved more powerfully than on the beachside. As he rowed, Allistair remembered Lord John saying he would leave DuPree Island in his capable hands while Daniel would assume his title and inherit the estate in England.

13

Would any of that change now that Lord John wanted his oldest child to come home? Was she already married? If so, would her husband want to take over?

Allistair knew the *1870 Married Women's Property Act* had failed to supply safeguards for married women. He also knew a further act passed in 1883 allowed women to buy and keep any property deemed separate from their husbands. They would receive the same legal protection as husbands if they needed to defend their rights to property.

What would happen to Allistair if Victoria decided to make sweeping changes?

Rowing as fast as he could, he decided to wait for Lord John to finish the rest of the story before worrying. Allistair remembered his father saying, "Don't borrow trouble from the future today."

After a warm bath, Allistair dressed for dinner before seeing if Lord John wanted to continue their conversation. He took a deep breath, then he knocked, and quickly pasted a smile on his face. He was prepared for Lord John to look worse. Instead, he was sitting up reading *The Times*. Lord John had finished his dinner, and a small brandy was on a bedside table.

"I am glad to see you, my son. I sat up for a while and saw you taking out a rowboat. You rowed so fast I thought you should join a rowing club on the mainland," Lord John said with a hearty laugh.

"I enjoyed my trip to the other side of the island. Rowing was a great way to clear my confusion. I came to see if you wanted to continue the story of your daughter," he said, giving Lord John's hand a quick squeeze.

"Yes, I have much to tell you. Pull up a chair, and after I am finished, please ask me any questions you have," Lord John said.

Allistair nodded to signal his consent; Lord John continued his unbelievable story of leaving his daughter in London.

"I wanted to make sure that Victoria wasn't put in an orphanage, so I pretended to be looking for a job, and while applying, I heard that the Montgomerys were going to adopt her since they could not have children of their own. That made the pain lessen a little. They were good people, and I knew they would treat Victoria as their own daughter, and she would lack for nothing.

"I tracked her through Rebecca's brother and sister-in-law, but as Victoria grew, I wanted to know more, so I planted someone in the household who could give me day-to-day details. I won't tell you who because, should Victoria decide to not come, I still want that person to keep me informed." Lord John reached for his brandy and took several sips.

"I know your daughter is almost twenty-one years old. Is she married? Does she have children?" Allistair asked, desperate to know where he stood.

"Victoria turns twenty-one next Friday. She isn't

married yet and doesn't have children. I have heard she is incredibly involved with helping unfortunate women and children in London and those on the Montgomery estate."

"Lord John, you must be proud of her willingness to help those less fortunate. Her adopted parents seem to have raised a well-brought-up young lady who cares a lot." Allistair was impressed with Victoria himself and glad she wasn't a disappointment to Lord John.

"Rebecca would be so pleased that Victoria shows compassion for others. She cared for the families living here on the island.

"I remember riding with Rebecca as she personally visited each family at Christmas. Seeing the children so excited was a highlight for her. They started speculating about the surprises that might be included in the baskets early in December," Allistair said, remember the event with a smile.

"I hope you understand why I need Victoria to finally come home. I must see her before I die. Are you sure you can take on this mission for me?" Lord John looked at him with tears in his eyes, as if hoping he would agree.

"Lord John, you know I regard you as my father. You took care of me and provided me a stable home when my mother withdrew into herself. I could never deny any request you make. I will take on this mission as well as request that Daniel come home.

"I understand your urgency, and with Victoria's birthday being next week, I will start planning my trip to London tonight. I will write notes to Daniel and Lord Montgomery. I will bring them to you tomorrow for review and will make any revisions you think necessary." Allistair patted Lord John's shoulder.

"Allistair, I need you to go to this address first. It's the address for a dressmaker. I want a gown and fan made for Victoria and delivered on her birthday. Put in the note to the Montgomerys that Victoria has a heart-shaped birthmark on her right shoulder. That will confirm that I am her birth father." Lord John finished his brandy.

"I will see you tomorrow with both notes," Allistair said, leaving to have his evening meal.

Within three days, he was on a ship headed to London. Allistair did not know what was ahead but valued Lord John's belief in him and would complete the mission.

The Montgomerys' London townhouse looked empty from the sidewalk when Allistair walked by, hoping to catch a glimpse of Victoria before he arrived on her birthday. Deciding to find out if they were in residence, Allistair knocked on the ornate wooden double doors. After the butler answered, Allistair presented his calling card and asked for Lord Montgomery.

"Sir, I am sorry, but the family is not in residence and will not be back for the rest of the Season," the butler informed him.

Later that night, Allistair visited White's Gentlemen's Club to find out the gossip about the Montgomerys, especially Victoria. He overheard somebody mention the family while he enjoyed a brandy. Moving closer, Allistair took a seat where he could better hear the conversation.

"I'm glad the Montgomerys decided to remove to the country ahead of time. Knowing a thug was looking for revenge against their daughter had to be very disturbing," said one gentleman sipping on his drink.

"I heard the scoundrel is furious that Miss Montgomery rescued his daughter from the hell she lived in. How could a father sell his own daughter to his friends and associates?" asked the other older gentleman.

After leaving the club, Allistair arrived back at the DuPree townhome where he was staying while in London. He was glad he knew where the Montgomerys were but distressed at the news that Victoria could be in danger.

Chapter Three:
Birthday Surprises

VICTORIA turned over and stretched her arms toward the ceiling, glad she had a refreshing night of sleep. A long day of preparation was ahead before her twenty-first birthday ball would begin. Knowing she needed to get up but wanting a few minutes to reflect on her life, she closed her eyes and thought about how lucky she was.

As an only child of a wealthy English couple, Lord Andrew and Lady Hannah Montgomery, Victoria had never wanted for anything. Her parents didn't spoil her, but she knew she was privileged after seeing how Sally lived in the slums of London.

Suddenly, the thought that money could buy whatever you wanted, including a baby, popped into her mind. She remembered the discussion with her mother a few weeks ago about Sally's infant almost being sold to a wealthy couple who could not have one.

Thinking about having children made Victoria realize the one thing missing in her life was having the right man to ask her to be his wife. She had admirers, of course, but no man had been "the one." Victoria's parents had not tried to force her into marriage; they were in love and wanted the same for her.

With social and charitable commitments filling her days, Victoria didn't think of marriage often. Her tutor taught her the skills needed for a young lady of her standing in society: sewing delicate silk embellishment, embroidery, playing the piano, and speaking in three languages, including English. But of all these accomplishments, Victoria enjoyed playing the piano the best.

Her parents encouraged her to consider the feelings of others when making decisions that could affect their lives. The injustices the lower classes faced daily affected her significantly. She saw the household staff more as friends than servants, which endeared her to them. Victoria worked with her mother to improve the staffs' lives and help their extended families as well. They always supplied baskets of food on holidays and special occasions such as a child's birthday. If possible, they made the deliveries in person. Whenever a new member joined the household staff, the Montgomerys found out if they could read and write, and if not, they saw to their education.

When Victoria was fourteen, Father taught her the workings of the estate. "Victoria, having this knowledge will be an immense help to your future husband," he had said, with pride that she understood everything quickly. They discussed all the aspects needed to make their endeavors prosperous for them and their staff. She learned how to balance the accounts and where to invest in new farming implementations. Father asked her opinion on housing, payments, and other living conditions for the farmworkers and other estate employees. As she became more knowledgeable, Father applied many of her recommendations for improvements and additions.

"Victoria, I know guests are boring at times," said Mother. "I did notice today, during Lady Randolph's visit with us, you tried to hide several yawns behind your teacup."

"But, Mother," Victoria moaned, "she is hard of hearing, repeats the same questions, and falls asleep often, but I tried to be social and welcoming."

"You are only fifteen, but you must learn to feign your interest in the conversations. This is good training for when you are mistress of your own home. I have decided you need a companion. There are times when I am not available to go shopping or attend social events with you. A companion will be an immense help in that respect. Don't worry, I will get someone close to your age," said Lady Hannah. "I realize being an only child has been lonely for you."

"Mother, I think that having a companion my age would be wonderful. Will you let me meet her before you offer her the position? I would like to see if we are compatible." Victoria hugged her mother, hoping the answer would be yes.

Two days later, Victoria met with Lady Hannah to discuss how the search was going.

"My friend, Lady Yolanda Stanford, knows of a young girl named Emma Jonas, who just completed a school for young ladies and is looking for a position as a companion. Lady Stanford said her brother-in-law is sponsoring Emma to help her secure employment. He said his young cousin and his cook's daughter shared the same tutor. The tutor gave Emma high praise and hoped she would be able to obtain an acceptable position in a good household," Lady Hannah said. "We have an interview with Emma this afternoon, and she is only five years older than you."

"I look forward to meeting her. I like that she has worked hard to better her station," Victoria said. All the other staff was older, and she was delighted to have someone with whom she could have more in common.

The interview was at three o'clock. Emma arrived ten minutes early, which pleased both Lady Hannah and Victoria. They settled in the parlor and enjoyed tea while they discussed what the position entailed.

"Emma, you come highly recommended," Lady Hannah said. "The letter from your finishing school included your scores which are above average. As you know, it isn't socially acceptable for a young lady to receive male visitors without her mother or a chaperone present. I need to know you will never let anyone overstep the boundaries."

"Lady Montgomery, I will take my responsibilities seriously. I know the proper etiquette for a young lady of high social standing and will be on guard against any wrongdoing by young men," Emma said.

After a half-hour, Lady Hannah excused herself. She said she would be back in a few minutes. Victoria knew she was giving them time to talk and get to know one another.

"Emma, are you originally from London?" Victoria asked.

"No, Miss Victoria. I am from southern England. I lived with my father and brother. My mother passed away a few years ago." One curl fell across her eyes when she bent her head as if remembering the pain of her mother's passing.

"I'm sorry about your mother. But do call me Victoria. If you become my companion, I will insist that you do." Victoria hoped her mother would offer the position to her.

When the interview was over, Lady Hannah told Emma she would contact her within two days.

"Victoria, what do you think of her?" Mother asked.

"I like her and think she would be perfect as my companion. Mother, will you offer her the position?" Victoria sat forward on the settee and waited for the answer.

Three days later, Emma moved into a room next to Victoria. After working as the companion for several months, Emma astutely pointed out that Victoria's maid wasn't efficient. The maid burned Victoria's hair several times and didn't make sure her gowns were free of wrinkles, so she talked with Lady Hannah and offered to take on that duty as well.

With Emma as her companion, Victoria no longer found social visits boring. After the guests left, they met in Victoria's room to discuss the fashions worn and the conversations. They shared the same sense of humor, laughed about outrageous outfits, and wondered if the stories told were true or just gossip. After Victoria's coming-out ball, she started receiving male visitors. Emma was always present and made sure everything was proper. She accompanied Victoria to social events with many late-night reminiscences. She also ate with the family, gave directions to servants, did fancy sewing when needed, and poured tea during social visits. Emma proved to be great company.

"Good morning, Victoria. I wish you a wonderful twenty-first birthday," Emma sang, while opening the drapes.

"Thank you, my friend. What a wonderful day for a party," Victoria said, looking out the floor-to-ceiling windows at the sunny vista.

Victoria's parents were hosting a ball at their country manor home to celebrate the happy occasion. Friends and relatives would soon arrive. Maids and servants had been transforming the gigantic hall into a ballroom even before daybreak. Gardeners filled the decorative centerpieces on the massive table in the dining room with large floral arrangements.

After breakfast, her mother and father asked her to come outside with them.

"We have a birthday surprise for you," Father said, leading Victoria to the side door.

An Arabian stallion was standing on the pathway to the stables. The horse was as black as night with a small white star on his forehead. Victoria could not help but run over to it. She had other horses growing up, but she could feel the connection with this stallion when he nuzzled her neck and whinnied such a soft sound, which only she heard.

Victoria's parents gave her a sky-blue riding habit featuring a hip-length jacket and trailing petticoats for riding sidesaddle. She also received presents from her friends and relatives who could not travel from London for the party: three pretty fans, a white shawl with diamond accents, an emerald headband, a diamond brooch, and other jewelry pieces.

Victoria's dressmaker had created a snow-white silk ballgown, leaving her shoulders bare. It gathered at the waist with a sash of gold, and the hem was embroidered with a deep panel of golden flowers. The skirt had an overlay of sheer fabric and was fuller in the back than in the front, which gracefully moved as she walked.

With such a wonderful family and good friends, how could anything go wrong? Just as she thought these words, someone knocked on her door.

"Victoria, you have received another gift," Emma informed her upon entering.

"Thank you. You can put the box on my bed."

When she left, Victoria went to see what was inside. She carefully opened the package exquisitely wrapped in blue paper.

Lying between the tissues was a gorgeous cerulean chiffon dress with an oval-shaped neckline trimmed in lace. The puffed sleeves ended with lace bands at the wrists as well. Pinned to the dress was a cameo brooch encircled with diamonds. Victoria rang for Emma to help her into the gown.

"Who sent this present? I don't see a note anywhere," asked Victoria, desperate to find out.

"If there wasn't a note in the box, I don't know," said Emma. "The boy who delivered the package did not leave a message either."

Victoria went to ask her mother if she knew anything about the mysterious gift.

"Mother," she called, "is this dress from you?"

"No, darling. The white one you're wearing tonight is the only dress I had made for you."

"Mother, if you didn't send it, who did?" she asked.

Victoria soon discovered Father had not sent it, nor had any other family members staying with them for the ball. Not knowing where the gift came from was exciting. What if she had a secret admirer? Needing to get ready for the ball, she tried to forget about the dress and went to her room to change.

As Victoria pulled on her white gloves, Emma knocked and brought in another wrapped gift. The first thing she noticed was the same blue wrapping paper.

There wasn't a note in the box, either.

With a shiver of anticipation, she carefully lifted out an exquisite fan with a mother of pearl handle. The feathers attached to it were the same blue as the dress she had received earlier.

Victoria ran down the hall to her parents' sitting room. She knocked a little harder than necessary because she knew she needed guidance and advice about keeping the gifts. Why wasn't there a note? Was there a hidden agenda behind this? Had somebody formed an attachment to her? A young lady could not accept gifts without her parents' consent. Keeping them would give the wrong impression.

"You may enter," Mother called. Dressed and ready for the party, she and Father were taking a few minutes to relax before a long night of entertaining friends and family. From their looks of confusion, she could tell they had something to say to her even before Victoria showed them the fan.

"Mother and Father, what is wrong? You both look worried. Do you know already about the second gift without a note? Are you aware of who sent them?"

A look she did not understand passed between her parents before her father asked her to sit beside her mother, who took her hand. Turning and walking across the room, as if he needed a minute to compose himself, Father seemed to struggle to find a way to tell her something.

"Please know: your mother and I love you with all of our hearts. You are the daughter we wished for but thought we would never have. We were not able to have children until you came, and we are older than most of your friends' parents. You are such a blessing to us, and we have cherished every minute we have had with you."

"I know you both love me, but I'm confused. What are you trying to tell me? You are making me worried." Victoria looked from her mother to her father.

"Sweetheart, you were adopted."

Chapter Four: Overwhelmed

ATHER'S last four words replayed in Victoria's head until a storm began to rage inside her. She could only think of the thwarted plan to sell Sally's baby to a wealthy couple who could not bear children. What if the same thing had happened to Victoria when she was a baby? Was she adopted through legal channels, or was she bought from an evil man as well? Did her mother use her affiliation with the unwed women's charity to buy Victoria?

Father began to speak, so Victoria had to pull herself back to the present and listen to what other revelations he would make about her. Could she endure more?

"Sweetheart, I am going to tell you something hard to believe, but it is true. Twenty years ago, your mother was returning from a night at the opera with your great aunt, Agnes, in our family coach. Your mother walked up the front steps of our townhouse. She saw a basket somebody had placed near the front door.

"Preparing to have the butler retrieve it, your mother paused when she heard a small whimper. When she saw the basket move, her curiosity grew. She thought a kitten might be inside, so she lifted the lid and instead saw a baby girl wrapped in clothing made of the finest blue material, as well as a note and a silver rattle. The quality of the paper and handwriting led us to believe somebody from a prominent family had left the child there."

"Please say nothing more. I don't want to know what else you have to tell me." Victoria clasped her hands over her ears.

Mother gently pulled down her daughter's hands and held them as Father continued. "The note instructed us to raise the baby as our own. The parents knew they could not keep the child because of a threat made to harm her. Fear led to the decision to give her up."

Tears ran down Hannah's face. "Victoria, you are the baby left on our doorstep all those years ago."

In complete disbelief, all Victoria could do was stare at her mother with her mouth agape. The word "adopted" instead of *bought* should have helped Victoria feel better. But until she knew the whole story, she wasn't sure how she felt.

"Your mother walked into my study, holding a baby. Before I could inquire where the infant came from, you reached for me. I took you in my arms, and you laid your cheek on my shoulder." Tears shone in Father's eyes, and his chin quivered.

"The note pinned to your blanket said your name was *Victoria* and gave the date of your birth which is today," said Mother, looking so melancholy.

"We tried to find your birth parents," continued Father. "After many inquiries by a private detective, he found a couple with a baby had been staying at Grosvenor Hotel but for only two days. No one saw a baby when they left the hotel to board a ship to Madagascar. The names listed on the manifest were Mr. and Mrs. Smith. The trail ended there because the vessel was stopping so often along the way, finding them would be almost impossible.

"Without finding any other clues about who and where your birth parents might be, your mother and I went to our family lawyer to get his advice on adopting you. We were determined that no matter how long or difficult the process might be, we would not give up until you were our daughter. We knew providence had left you on our doorstep ...."

Mother silently cried as Father continued with the story.

"Why are you just now telling me this on my birthday?" Victoria said, in an irritated tone. She didn't know whether she was angry or stunned but needed them to know she was upset.

"Years ago, we agreed to wait until the day after your twenty-first birthday to tell you about the adoption. We knew it would upset you no matter when you found out that you were left on our doorstep but felt you would better understand when you turned twenty-one," Mother added.

31

"I have more to tell you that you need to know." Father moved over to stand in front of Victoria and took her hand.

"My mind is overwhelmed with what you have told me already. I don't know if I can handle any more." Victoria's lower lip trembled.

"After all these years, it seems your birth father wants to see you," Father said, as sadness clouded his features.

"What?" Victoria snatched her hand from his. Suddenly, she was mentally drained. All she had heard was so hard to believe.

"Sorry, Father, for speaking so loudly, but I hope I misheard what you said." Victoria's voice was still shrill.

"Minutes ago, we received a note from somebody named Allistair DuPree. He wrote saying you are his fourth cousin, and he is on his way here to meet you. He also sent you the anonymous gifts from your birth father, Lord John DuPree. He wrote that your birth father wants you to come to the family island. This part is hard to tell you, but your birth father has cancer and does not have long to live."

Victoria's body went cold with dread. All she could do was sit there, stupefied. Could any of this be true?

Left on a doorstep as a baby.

Adopted by the Montgomerys.

Now her birth father wanted to see her before he died.

"This is too much. Within a few minutes, my whole life as I knew it has been swept away. How do you keep such a secret for so long from someone you claim to love? Isn't love based on honesty, respect, and trust?" Victoria asked, her jaw ached from clenching her teeth tight, trying not to scream her frustration.

"Based on the note saying you were in danger; we didn't want you to find your birth parents at a younger age if it meant you could be hurt. We knew you would be more mature at twenty-one and could handle the truth then. Please don't judge your birth parents or us too harshly. We have done what we believe was best for you," Mother said.

"I am sorry for losing my temper. You have been the best parents, and I know you only want my happiness. I am hurt and angry, but most of all, I want answers. I will ask Mr. DuPree to tell me all he knows. Who tried to hurt me? Why have they waited till now to contact me?" Victoria put her head in her hands.

"Victoria, Allistair DuPree insists that he has proof what he says is true. He knows you have a heart-shaped birthmark on your back near your right shoulder blade. Only your mother and I and Emma know about your birthmark.

"I will meet with him first and find out what he has to say. Then I will ask you to come to my study if I believe his story and see his proof. If I do not ask you to come down before the ball, then I will come to your room to let you know nothing came of his claim."

Father saw from Victoria's face she was astonished by his tale.

"Don't worry; all will work out," said Father. "You will always be our daughter. You don't have to decide tonight, dear. Mr. DuPree's note indicated he would be in England for two weeks. If you want to see your birth father after that, he will be your escort along with any servants you wish to take. I will help make all the arrangements," Father said, with a clearing of the throat.

A knock sounded on the door. "Lord Montgomery, Mr. Allistair DuPree is downstairs asking for you," said the butler.

"Thank you, I will be down momentarily," Lord Andrew said, dismissing him.

Mother stood, pulling Victoria up beside her, and wrapped her in a warm tight embrace. Victoria's mind could not think with all the emotions and questions tumbling around in there, so she pushed them aside, afraid she would collapse to the floor. Her father appeared older now, while her mother looked so weary.

"Oh, Mother, I have left tear stains on your silk dress. You had it made for the ball tonight."

"Do not worry, my dear. I will wear the shawl that goes with it, and no one will be the wiser." Mother's face wilted. "Run along now. I know you have many questions but wash your face and wait for your father to either summon you or come to your room to let you know what Mr. DuPree has to say."

As Victoria turned to leave, she asked if they should continue with the ball?

"Yes," Mother said, straightening her back. "We have many guests staying here with us. Local friends and family are already on their way, so we can't stop now; not on your special day."

Victoria turned to close the door and heard her

mother run to her father.

"Andrew, do you think she hates us for not telling her earlier? She is my baby girl, and I can't lose her," Hannah said, in a voice laced with worry.

Victoria knew her father would soothe her fears. He more than likely pulled her in his arms. Victoria didn't stay to hear any more of their private conversation. Instead, she slowly walked back to her rooms.

Victoria applied cream to hide the redness under her eyes, and waited, fighting visions of herself being sold like Sally's baby. She now felt such a connection to the poor girl. Within thirty tense minutes, Emma arrived to tell her that Father wanted her to come to his study. Rising from her favorite reading chair, she smoothed out any wrinkles in her skirts.

"Victoria, you look so sad. Can I help?" Emma asked.

"Sweet friend, I am sad. I just found out the Montgomerys adopted me. Now my birth father is dying and wants to see me. Oh, I don't know what to do.

"Did you know about the adoption?" Victoria looked her best friend in the eyes. She would know if Emma told her a lie.

"I did not know. None of the staff ever mentioned it to me. I only joined the household when I was fifteen," Emma reminded her.

35

"I am your friend, and you know you can tell me anything. Over the years, we have always kept our confidences and secrets, and that will always be the case," Emma said, giving Victoria a quick hug.

She realized Father believed that Allistair DuPree was her cousin, confirming that this nightmare was real. However, she wanted to appear as calm as possible when she met him for the first time, so she squared her shoulders and lifted her chin.

Chapter Five: Decision Time

*V*ICTORIA started to run down the stairs but checked herself. Slowly she made her way to find out if other secrets and unknowns awaited her. She was anxious as she knocked on the door of Father's study and entered.

Father took several steps toward her from where he had been standing near the fireplace, then he looked to his left. Seated in one of the leather-bound chairs near the desk was the most handsome man Victoria had ever seen.

The man rose to his feet and stared at her as if seeing a ghost. He then gave her a smile with even white teeth that made Victoria weak in the knees. She was at a loss for words. His hair was as black as a raven, unfashionably long with a slight wave. She had the sudden urge to push back the piece that kept falling across his left eye. Where did this urge come from? She had never thought of the opposite sex that way before. He stood over six feet tall and had the incredible physique of somebody who spends a lot of time outdoors. He had a chiseled jawline and aristocratic nose, which gave him the appearance of a romance novel's hero, but his most unique feature was his startling cerulean-blue eyes.

Victoria was unable to move, so Father walked over, took her elbow, and led her to the settee to the right of his desk.

"Victoria, may I present your cousin, Allistair DuPree. He wants to tell you about your birth family."

Still in disbelief, Victoria slowly shook her head, distrustful of what she would hear, but she needed to know. Finding her voice, at last, she asked Mr. DuPree to have a seat in the chair to her right. Her father sat beside her, taking her small cold hand in his much larger one.

"Miss Montgomery, please call me Allistair since we are distant relatives. I am sorry that my visit must come as a surprise to you. But you will understand everything once you know that your birth parents did not abandon you. They knew they had no other choice to save your life."

Victoria waited to hear what he had to say before letting her emotions take control. She sat with her back as straight as an arrow, raised her chin, and clutching her hands together.

Allistair shifted in his chair. "To preface what I am going to tell you, I was completely unaware that you were alive until a few days ago.

"Your birth parents' names are Lord John DuPree and Lady Rebecca Stanford."

Victoria released a deep-held breath; when Allistair mentioned Rebecca Stanford, she was surprised. They were friends of her parents and had been a constant in her life since childhood. Were they related to her? Did they know that she was Rebecca's daughter?

Looking at her father, she could see he questioned his friends' connection also. Before she could ask, Allistair settled his gaze upon her and continued.

"Your father, Lord John, took over most of the day-to-day operation of the wheat farming on the island where we live until he fell ill. Wheat is the island's chief crop, and we employ many servants and farmworkers. We also raise horses."

Victoria scooted forward with a small gasp of excitement that she immediately tried to suppress. Father patted her arm. "My daughter adores horses. She has been able to ride almost before she could walk."

Allistair seemed to relish Victoria's enthusiasm. "We raise and train them for the Grand National and other racing events throughout Europe. When I finished university, I returned to the island and took over your father's duties when he got sick. . . ."

Why had he not revealed anything else about her birth mother? Victoria raised her hand to get his attention before he could continue.

"Allistair, why haven't you mentioned Rebecca? Did something happen to her?"

"Two years after you were left in London, your mother died giving birth to your brother, Daniel," he answered, lowering his head.

39

Victoria could see Rebecca's death still affected him after all these years. Slowly, tears slid down her face, tears for a mother she would never know. Allistair reached out his hand toward her as if to give her comfort.

After she gained her composure, Allistair continued, "I need to back up and tell you about your parents leaving you in London. As I said, the first two years living on the island were full of love and laughter for them. Lord John and Lady Rebecca were so excited the day they found out they were having a baby. I was seven by then and looked forward to having a playmate living in the manor.

"After your birth, things began to change. Your mother refused to leave you with a nanny or even your grandmother. I only heard whispers, and the conversations always came to a stop whenever I went into the room. I don't know everything, but an attempt to kill you happened a couple of months before you were ten months old."

At this revelation, Victoria shivered as a chill crept over her spine.

"I do know when you began to crawl, Lord John took a business trip to Cardiff, Wales. Rebecca decided that you and she would go with him. Their journey began in London so they could introduce you to your mother's family. Returning to the island from Wales, Lord John informed the family that you died from a fever you caught on board the ship. Burial was at sea. Your mother was so distraught and stayed in her rooms most of the time. I remember I was upset and cried late at night. That was the first time I knew someone so young who died," Allistair admitted.

"Until they found out she was going to have another baby, she rarely ventured out of their suite of rooms."

Jumping to her feet, Victoria walked across the room to distance herself from such awful revelations. After a minute, she took a deep breath with a head shake then turned back to Allistair.

"I know you said my birth parents loved me," spat Victoria, but how could they construct a lie that surely brought such grief and sorrow? Everyone must have been distraught at the news. I know I am almost speechless."

"They knew the only way to keep you safe was to declare you dead," said Allistair. "Lord John said he wants to tell you the rest of the story and show you portraits of your mother. He also wants to introduce you to your brother, Daniel. He is on his way home from Oxford. He doesn't know his older sister is alive, but I'm sure he will be thrilled."

Victoria went from anger, that they had lied about her death, to delight at the news that she had a sibling. Her emotions were all over the place. She could feel a headache developing at the base of her neck.

"I have a brother?" Victoria's pulse raced. "Growing up an only child, I always wanted a brother." She looked at Lord Montgomery and gave him a hug to apologize for being happy to have a sibling.

"Victoria, if you decide not to come to see him, Lord John will send you a letter with all the details, but he wants to tell you in person."

She gripped Father's handkerchief, now soaked with

her tears, as if it were a lifeline. She knew time was passing so quickly and had heard the butler already greeting some early guests.

"Allistair, I have to say, I have been told so many astonishing revelations in the last hour or so that I can't think straight. Thank you for coming on Lord John's behalf. I am glad you will be in England for two weeks so I can ask questions about the DuPree family and find out more about the island before I can make a decision."

Father had been quiet most of the time but spoke up now. "Mr. DuPree, I know you traveled here before securing accommodations. My wife and I invite you to stay with us while you are in England. Victoria can tell you about her life here and ask questions about the DuPree family also."

Standing, Victoria turned to Allistair and extended her hand. "I do hope you will stay, and you must join us for the ball."

Tingles traveled over her body when their hands made contact. She looked into Allistair's eyes and could see he felt it, too. Slowly, he released her hand and gave her the most stunning smile she had ever seen, intensifying the blue in his eyes.

Hurriedly, Victoria took the back staircase to her room to freshen up before joining her guests. Having fun seemed so trivial now that she knew the truth about herself, but canceling the ball was not an option.

Allistair stood and watched Victoria walk away. She glanced back at him with sparkling hazel eyes that, for a second, seemed to look into his soul. Her voice was melodious with a touch of rawness. To him, she was a vision in white. Petite in stature, her figure was perfect, and her curves filled out her clothes nicely. Her breasts were full, and her waist slim. Her golden-blond curls, styled in an elaborate updo with two ringlets left free, perfectly framed her heart-shaped face.

The touch of her delicate fingers had been so acute it aroused all his senses. What was happening to him? He had just met Victoria, and this might be the only time he would ever see her because she might decide to stay in England.

Emma was waiting for Victoria in her room. She looked lovely in her gown and was already swaying to the faint sound of the orchestra music coming from the ballroom.

"Victoria, I need to go check on your dancing shoes being shined for the ball. I will return in a minute," Emma said, after adding the finishing touches to Victoria's hair.

As Emma opened the door, she came to a sudden stop. From where Victoria sat at her vanity, she could see the look of bewilderment on Emma's face, which she quickly covered with her hand, releasing a small gasp. Victoria glanced out the door and saw Allistair with the same look of surprise on his face. His hand was on the doorknob of a bedroom across the hall. Hearing the noise of Victoria's door opening caused him to turn their way.

"Emma, what is wrong?" she asked, getting to her feet. Allistair saw Victoria and walked over.

"Ladies, I'm sorry I startled you," he said.

"Allistair, let me introduce you to my companion, Emma Jonas."

"Emma, this is Allistair DuPree. He is a guest staying for a few weeks," she informed her.

"Hello, Emma. It's nice to meet you." Allistair bowed and turned to walk back across the hall. He raised his hand with a slight wave and softly closed his bedroom door.

Chapter Six:
Dancing the Night Away

VICTORIA tried to push everything to the back of her mind as she took her father's arm and entered the ballroom. They walked to the dais, where the musicians were softly playing. Father signaled to them to stop so he could address the crowd.

"Thank you for coming to help celebrate this special day. Twenty-one years ago, a rosy-cheeked baby girl made us a complete family." He gestured for Mother to join them. With his arm around both Victoria and Hannah, he continued to tell everyone how proud they were of Victoria. She could not keep a tear from rolling down her right cheek as everyone clapped.

Father signaled for the musicians to play again before leading her to the floor for the first dance. Twirling around, she noticed Allistair standing near the open balcony doors. He wore a black superfine dress coat, a pair of well-fitting pants, a vest, and a cravat all the same color. A white linen cambric handkerchief was the finishing touch to his ensemble. The wayward curl kept falling over his forehead. He saw Victoria looking his way and raised his hand in acknowledgment. She could feel a faint blush warm her cheeks.

Tonight was a night to dance, and tomorrow was soon enough to face the future. Victoria planned to enjoy herself and cherish the company of her family and friends. She did not have a minute to think as she went from one guest to another. As soon as she caught her breath, someone was asking her to dance.

Minutes before midnight, Allistair finally invited her to join him in a waltz, which meant they could talk. Tongue-tied at first, not only because of his good looks, but she still could not believe how her life was changing.

"Miss Montgomery, thanks for inviting me to your birthday ball. I know how hard this must be for you, but you have such wonderful parents and friends here tonight." He moved elegantly and led her around the dance floor with ease.

She looked up and noticed his eyes were the same shade of cerulean blue as the mystery gifts. The lighting in Father's study had not been bright enough to reveal the brilliant hue, but under the chandelier light in the ballroom, she could see the actual color.

"Call me Victoria," she said, slightly tripping over her feet. "Sorry, I usually don't stumble when I dance, but I think everything is finally catching up with me." She could tell Allistair was pleased she had asked him to call her by her first name, but he did not have time to say anything. As their dance came to an end, a gong sounded, signaling the evening meal was ready.

"May I escort you to dinner," Allistair asked, offering his arm. She lightly placed her hand on his coat sleeve as they walked through the dining room doors.

Selecting a table, she sat down while Allistair went to the buffet to get them some food. The dining room and several adjacent rooms were set up with small tables for guests. Everyone seemed famished after all the dancing and from playing cards in the parlor.

Mother had spent days choosing the menu. The buffet consisted of white soup made with veal stock, cream, and almonds; cold meats, such as chicken or sliced ham; poached salmon; glazed carrots and other seasonal vegetables; salads; and fresh fruits. There were also several types of biscuits, elaborately decorated cakes, and a wide variety of cheeses, pies, and trifles. Tea, coffee, lemonade, white wine claret, and red wines were available for those thirsty. Gentlemen could have port to enjoy with their cigars.

Returning to the table, Allistair carried two plates overflowing with all manner of delicacies. He put one plate in front of her before going to get them something to drink.

Victoria did not know she was so hungry until she looked down at her almost empty plate. With an unspoken agreement, they did not discuss her decision about going to the island.

"Allistair, my parents gave me a stallion for my

birthday. I hope you can join me for a ride later this week." Victoria had learned to ride while still a small child, and other than playing the piano, riding was her favorite pastime.

"I accept your invitation to go riding with you, and I might challenge you to a race, but I have to warn you I always win," Allistair said with a small laugh.

Since she was the birthday girl, they did not spend too much time in the dining room. She needed to make sure her guests were enjoying themselves. Leaving his side at the entrance of the ballroom, she saw her mother's small wave and made her way over to her.

Mother seemed worried. Victoria assured her she was enjoying herself.

Two hours later, her feet hurt from dancing, but her adrenaline was high. So much had happened in the last few hours. The remaining guests had left as the sun was rising. Those staying in their guest rooms had gone up to bed after the final dance of the night.

As maids cleared the tables in the dining room, Mother and Father walked over to where she was resting in one of the alcoves created for conversation.

"Victoria, I hope you had a wonderful time tonight," said her father.

"I'm exhausted, but such a magical evening shouldn't have to end." Smiling, she looked at her mother and could see such sadness on her face.

"Victoria, you should go to bed. Tomorrow we will have plenty of time to talk. Mr. DuPree went to his room about an hour ago. All of us need clear heads before making any decisions, and tomorrow will be soon enough to face what lies ahead. Good night."

Victoria slowly made her way up the staircase. When she reached the landing, she looked down and saw her parents embrace. Then hand in hand, they walked into the parlor. At that moment, she made a birthday wish that she would find love and friendship as they had.

A sound from below caused her to look down into the foyer again. She saw one of the servants, hired for the party, looking up at her with hatred on his face. Victoria's body went cold with dread. What if he was Sally's father or one of his unsavory friends from London who had found her?

The man moved toward Victoria, where she stood transfixed. She didn't realize she had yelled "Stop" until her parents reappeared.

Lord Andrew looked to where Victoria was on the landing and saw the expression of fear on her face. He turned to find the source of the disturbance and saw the hired servant.

"What are you doing? Isn't your work here finished? Let me ring for the butler to pay you for your services tonight."

The man didn't glance at Lord Andrew; instead, he kept walking determinedly toward Victoria.

"I need you to wait in the kitchen for your payment, then you can leave," Lord Andrew said, with a gritting of his teeth. "Stop where you are!"

Allistair DuPree appeared on the landing above Victoria. "Lord Andrew, may I be of assistance?" He slowly walked down and stood in front of Victoria, using his body as a shield if necessary. "I do believe Lord Montgomery asked you to go to the kitchen. I suggest you do as you were told."

The servant charged toward Allistair, who moved with deliberate steps down the stairs. The man didn't say anything as he raised his fist to strike. The hit didn't connect because Allistair anticipated it and moved at the last second.

The servant stumbled from his own momentum, recovered quickly, and seemed to realize he wasn't prepared to take on Allistair, so he turned and tried to run past Lord Montgomery to make his escape.

Lord Montgomery stepped in front of the fleeing servant to stop him, but the man knocked him to the marble floor as if he were a rickety chair. Lady Montgomery screamed as blood poured from her husband's head.

Allistair sprinted past Lord Andrew and tried to catch the escaping man, who fled through one of the remaining open doors leading to the gardens. Returning in seconds, empty-handed, Allistair saw Lady Hannah holding her handkerchief to the wound on her husband's head. The butler and housekeeper appeared and began offering aid.

The butler summoned a doctor. By the time he arrived, two servants had helped Lord Andrew to his bedroom. After examining him, the doctor said the head wound was superficial. He recommended two days of bed rest, then Lord Andrew would be back to normal.

After the doctor left, servants moved a daybed into

Lord Andrew's room so Lady Hannah could be near should her husband need anything.

A search in and around the manor revealed the man was long gone. None of the staff knew who he was. The butler hired the rogue servant and others from the surrounding area to serve the many guests attending the birthday celebration.

Escorting Victoria into the parlor, Allistair asked if she was okay.

"I am better now, knowing Father isn't seriously hurt. Allistair, thank you for your help," Victoria said. "I can't imagine what would have happened if you had not appeared when you did. My parents are older, and the man could have easily subdued them."

"Victoria, I'm glad I hadn't gone to bed. I was reviewing paperwork when I heard Lord Andrew shouting," Allistair said. "I wish I could have caught the man. I'm glad your father wasn't hurt worse."

"Allistair, let's sit here for a minute. I need to tell you about a threat made to me after I helped a poor defenseless girl in London.

"I am on the board of directors for an unwed women's home where I help raise funds for the many services the home provides. A few months ago, I met Sally, a fourteen-year-old whose father abused her by selling her to his friends. She was with child, and he planned to sell the baby when it was born. I knew I had to help her escape that life. I was afraid, but I would do it again," Victoria said.

"We moved to the country two months earlier than

usual when we heard Sally's father had found out it was me who took his daughter away. He has promised to find me and make me pay. I am almost certain the man tonight is either Sally's father or one of his many unsavory associates."

"Victoria, you need to be careful. I believe your assumption is correct. When I arrived in London a few days ago, I overheard several men talking about your family at my gentlemen's club. I moved closer and heard them say a thug was looking for you because you stole his daughter. If you see anything unusual or any person who seems suspicious, let your father or me know."

"Do you think he found me all the way out here in the country?" Victoria asked.

"Yes, I do fear. Servants and staff always talk, add a little money to the equation, and Sally's father would know the location of your family estate in no time at all. I don't mean to scare or pressure you, but going to DuPree Island might be your best choice."

Chapter Seven:
Being Followed

ICTORIA tossed and turned for a long time, going over the day's events. At last, she concluded that she had to know who she was and remove the threat to the Montgomerys by Sally's father. Victoria decided to use the next two weeks to find out as much as possible from Allistair before letting everyone know about her *need* to go to DuPree Island to meet her father. After she came to her decision, she fell into a deep and troubled slumber.

When Victoria awoke, the sun was extra-golden behind the lace sheers. She rang for Emma and asked for breakfast in her room. She did not want to face anyone for a while.

"Victoria, I'm sorry your birthday ended with Lord Andrew being accosted by one of the hired men looking for more money. I'm glad his wound wasn't worse,"

Emma said, with sympathy in her voice. "Also, the staff asked me to let you know they enjoyed helping make your birthday a memorable event. They loved it when you met with them in the kitchen to personally thank them for their help. Giving everyone an extra day off this month was a wonderful gesture," Emma said, returning to remove the breakfast dishes.

Not wanting to worry the staff too much, Victoria and Allistair had told the butler that the man who hurt Lord Andrew was trying to extort more money for helping at the ball. When he was told that he was paid a fair salary, he struck Lord Andrew, who fell and hit his head.

Victoria dressed for the day and tried to convince herself that she was doing the right thing, but she still had doubts. As she opened the door to go downstairs, her mother was raising her hand to knock.

"Darling, how are you? Do you want to discuss yesterday's revelations?"

"Mother," she cried, throwing herself into her arms. "You will always have a special place in my heart." They stood there for a few minutes. Victoria wanted to retain the memory of how her mother felt and the sweet scent of her perfume. Arm in arm, they went to see Father in his bedroom.

"Good morning. I was so worried last night. I can see good color in your face, which I hope means you are feeling better this morning. Thank you again for my wonderful birthday celebration. I had such an enjoyable time." Smiling to add weight to her words, Victoria walked over and kissed his cheek.

"Love, I do feel well this morning. Your mother is making me stay in bed for two days, but I understand how worried everyone was last night. I wish it hadn't happened to spoil such a beautiful night. I loved seeing the joy on your face as you swirled around the dance floor. I am glad you didn't let the adoption news nor the run-in with the hired servant spoil your birthday," he said.

"Father, both have caused my mind to reel. Finding out about the adoption and meeting Allistair are almost unbelievable, but I knew worrying last night wouldn't change anything. I think Sally's father knows where I am. That worries me the most. I don't want anything to happen to you and Mother because of me."

Lord Andrew tried to convince Victoria that they would be on the lookout for anyone suspicious on the estate, and everyone would be safe. Victoria wasn't so sure and knew she would do anything to keep the Montgomerys safe, even if she had to move many miles away.

Drained from last night's celebration, everyone decided to spend the day relaxing before getting ready for dinner. Allistair had left earlier in the day to visit friends living close by.

On the ride to visit his friends who lived close to the

Montgomery estate, Allistair remembered how he was surprised at his reaction to meeting Victoria yesterday. The odds were not in his favor that she felt the same instant connection or even thought of him other than the man who turned her world upside down, but for him, that was not the case. He could not help but remember every second of their time together. Holding her in his arms as they danced the waltz gave Allistair the feeling of being where he belonged. When he awoke that morning, he could have sworn he could smell honeysuckle and oranges. He remembered the fragrance of Victoria's hair from last night when he danced with her.

Thinking of Victoria, he didn't sleep as soundly as he had hoped. He admired her involvement with the unfortunate young girl but was worried she was in danger from her heroic deed. He would keep a close eye on Victoria and hoped she would decide to go to the island, not only to meet Lord John but to remove herself from the reach of Sally's father.

Over the next week, Victoria spent as much time with Allistair as possible. She wanted to know more about Lord John, her brother, Daniel, and DuPree Island. Some of the stories made her cry, while others were so funny her sides hurt from laughing. She could tell he loved his family, now her family, very much.

"Allistair, you mentioned the Stanfords. My parents are friends with them. I have been to their home in London for several events. Do they know about me?"

"Victoria, I am the only one who knows you were adopted. Lord John won't let anyone else know until you decide if you are planning to come to the island."

Victoria tried to paint him a picture of her life in the country. She shared that being able to ride over open fields was her favorite part of being on the Montgomery estate. "If you wish, I would like to show you my favorite place to go when I need to gather my thoughts. There's a huge tree next to the river on the east side of the Montgomery estate. I have watched it grow from a sapling to a mighty tree."

"I would be honored," Allistair replied. "Maybe tomorrow will be the perfect day."

For the two weeks that Allistair planned to stay, Mother made sure dinner was only for the four of them. They learned more about the DuPree family during these informal meals, and Father entertained Allistair with stories about Victoria. His pride in her charitable endeavors and kind acts was evident and made her heart full. Some stories were funny, some embarrassing.

". . . Victoria was the cutest little girl. She would prance around dressed in her mother's pearls and heels." He got such a pensive look on his face.

"I will always be your little girl," she said, reaching for her father's hand.

As they were leaving the breakfast room the next morning, Victoria asked Allistair, "Are you available this morning to join me for a ride? I want to show you that special place here on the estate that means so much to me."

"Certainly, I will meet you at the stables in thirty minutes," he said.

Victoria was in her room, preparing to change into her riding habit when her mother knocked and came inside.

"Mr. DuPree is waiting for you in the library," said Mother. "He needs to know your decision about going to the island. A message arrived a few minutes ago saying Lord John's health has taken a turn for the worse. Mr. DuPree needs to get back to the island as soon as possible.

"Your father and I know you must go. We hope you will be safer on the island than here. We are certain Sally's father or one of his friends from London was at your birthday ball. Being on DuPree Island should make it much harder to find you. We give you our blessing and understand. Do you need me to send my maid to help Emma pack?" she asked.

"No, thank you. I think Emma will be all the help I need. May I ask her to go with me as my companion? I need someone with me whom I know and trust," she asked.

As Mother reached to open the bedroom door to leave, she cupped a hand over her mouth to keep from crying out; instead, she only nodded her acquiescence.

Victoria rang for Emma and asked her if she wanted to go with her to DuPree Island.

"I look forward to going, and I know I will have a great adventure," Emma agreed, with a mysterious look on her face.

Victoria left her to pack and slowly walked toward a new life. Opening the door to the library, she saw Allistair sitting in a chair with his head in his hands. Victoria's heart ached for him. She knew that her birth father's illness had put a strain on this handsome man sitting before her. She had the strangest feeling that she should somehow offer comfort to him. Her emotions confused her.

So deep in thought, Allistair had not heard her enter the room at first, but he soon seemed to sense that someone had come in. Raising his head, he saw her standing before him and gave her one of his brilliant smiles, which caused her heart to beat faster.

"Hello, Allistair. I spoke with Mother; she let me know that Lord John is much worse. I guess our ride will have to wait," she said softly.

"I'm sorry, but I need to prepare for the return trip to DuPree Island. I also must write to several business associates here in England that I was going to meet with later this week.

"I am so worried about Lord John's health. I hope you have come to tell me you will go with me," he said, standing to his feet with a look of hope that she would agree to accompany him.

"Allistair, I have made up my mind to go with you to see him. I'm also going so Sally's father won't be able to easily find me. Emma is packing for me now. She has agreed to go as my companion. If possible, we need to leave early in the morning because I am afraid that I might not get to see him before—"

"I was going to suggest the same to you. I will be ready to leave as soon as you are in the morning," Allistair replied.

Needing time to think, Victoria decided to go to her special place. She saddled her horse and left without telling anyone or taking a maid or a groom. Within a few minutes of riding, Victoria realized it was stupid to go by herself with the man who wanted to hurt her still at large, but she didn't want to turn around. She could already feel the anxiety dissolving with the wind flowing past her as she galloped.

She sat under her favorite tree next to the river. It always calmed Victoria's spirit. The slow flow of the river gave her peace. She pulled her knees up to her chest and rested her head on them. How long she remained that way, she didn't know, but suddenly she heard the dull rhythm of hooves against the soft earth.

Victoria raised her head to see Allistair had found her. He dismounted from his horse and sat down beside her. "Your parents were worried about you. When your horse wasn't in the stables, I told them I knew where you had gone. I explained that you had planned to show me your special place this morning and had told me where it was located."

When he reached for her hand, Victoria started to cry again. He pulled her to his shoulder and patted her back as sobs shook her petite frame. After regaining her composure, she sat upright.

"Allistair, I'm sorry for crying on your shirt," she said, wiping the remaining tears from her cheeks. "I'm glad you were the one to find me. I believe you, out of everyone, understand why I needed to come here."

"Victoria, you can talk to me about anything. I realize this is a difficult situation for you but trust me; I am here for you." Allister rested back against the tree.

"I want to see my birth father before the opportunity to build a relationship with him is too late. However, I am afraid about meeting the rest of the family and everyone else on the island. I don't know who put my life in jeopardy when I was a baby, but what if that person still wants to harm me?" she said, with a quiver in her voice.

"You don't have to worry. Your father and everyone else will love you. I will be there, so don't be afraid that somebody will try to attack you." Allistair leaned forward and kissed the top of her head, then wrapped his arms around her.

Their feelings were palpable, but they knew now was not the time to pursue them. They had to get the meeting with Lord John behind them first.

They left after breakfast the next day. Victoria was sad as she told her family goodbye.

"Mother and Father, you have made me the person I am today. I love you more than I can say and promise to come back for a visit soon. I will write weekly and let you know everything."

As they traveled, Victoria asked Allistair to tell her more about DuPree Island. "I know from Father the island is somewhere in the North Sea close to the mouth of the River Thames, but I do not know which route we will take to get there."

"Our trip will take eight hours by carriage from St. Albans to Southland-on-Sea, which is located where the Thames empties into the North Sea. From there, we will hire a boat and travel about ten miles out to sea," Allistair said. "Two other islands are located close to us. Neither one is as large as DuPree Island. The one located east of us is Black Rock, a deserted island. The closest one is Black Swan Island. Sir Samuel Wadsworth and his daughter, Laura, own that island and have a grand manor home on the shore of a large lake. Laura is the same age as your brother, Daniel. I am sure you will become friends in no time at all."

Victoria had never gone this far before. Allistair told her they were traveling during the day because highwaymen robbed carriages more readily after dark.

Before noon, they stopped at a reputable coaching inn to change horses and take refreshments. Victoria looked out the coach window as they drove away and noticed a man glaring at her. She could have sworn it was the same man who attacked her father. Should she tell Allistair? She might be wrong, so she decided to keep quiet. After the incident on the night of her birthday ended with Lord Andrew being hurt, she thought Allistair might knock the man out first then ask questions.

Even though they stopped several times to change horses and take refreshments, Victoria was bone tired when they reached the outskirts of Southland-on-Sea.

Darkness had fallen long before they boarded a ship that traveled eastward.

Victoria was thankful the distant piano music muffled her yawn on the upper deck. "Being on such a large ship is a new experience for me. I'm used to rowboats. I hope I don't get seasick. Emma, are you okay?"

"I've never gotten sick at sea before, so I think I'll be good," Emma said. "I will go check on our baggage to make sure it's secure."

"Are you cold, Victoria? We can go into the lounge. We only have a short time till we get to the island," said Allistair, searching for any sign of her discomfort.

"Thanks, but I'm enjoying the sea breeze. The waves

are hypnotic at night," said Victoria.

"When I got over the surprise of you being alive, Lord John asked me to go to London and have those gifts made for your birthday. He recommended a dressmaker. She knew who you were and said she had just made a ballgown for you. Did they meet with your approval?"

"Yes, very much. The dress fits perfectly and is magnificent. Why was it, the fan, and the wrapping paper made in that specific color of cerulean blue, may I ask? I noticed your eyes are that color, too."

"When you were born, your mother had all your clothes made with material in that color because it's the eye color of all the men born in the DuPree family. Cerulean is believed to be derived from a word meaning 'heaven's sky'—the color of the sky where it embraces the sea's horizon and seems to go for eternity."

Victoria fell silent because she wanted to think about everything that was going to happen to her. She was excited but afraid also.

Chapter Eight: Coming Home

THEY REACHED the island after one o'clock in the morning. Victoria was weary, but once she stepped out onto the sandy shore, her heart began to beat fast. She knew it sounded weird, but she felt like she had come home. She was only ten months old when taken to London, but she was sure she recognized the island's sights, sounds, and smells.

Victoria was nervous and almost fainted from anxiety. She would have fallen if Allistair had not reached out and taken her hand to encourage her to move forward.

"Victoria, the manor is a short climb up from the beach," Allistair said, stifling a yawn.

A boardwalk leading to a slight incline led toward the manor. Victoria could barely see the outline of a large home in front of her with only a torchlight illuminating the grand wooden doors. The butler was waiting outside the entry as soon as they reached it.

"Higgins, this is Miss Victoria Montgomery," Allistair announced, while showing her into the great hall.

Suspended from a high-beamed ceiling, two gleaming crystal chandeliers supplied light to showcase the home of a significant and prosperous family. Victoria noticed how haggard she looked in the massive mirror over the grand fireplace. Allistair led her to an elaborately furnished reception room similarly beamed as the hall but with richly paneled walls. A carpet in muted shades of gold, maroon, and royal blue softened the highly polished wood floor. A tea service was waiting for them.

"Shall I pour you a cup?" Victoria asked.

"That would be nice; thank you."

"I am excited to be here. So much has happened in the last week, but I'm glad you have been here to give me support." Victoria tried to focus through heavy eyelids.

Allistair pulled a silk cord near the fireplace. "I have summoned a maid who is waiting to show you to your rooms. I will introduce you to your father in the morning."

"Victoria, this is Clare. She'll help you tonight. Let her know if you need anything," said Allistair. "Now, if you will excuse me, I must finish some paperwork needing my attention before I retire for the night." Allistair took her hand and seemed reluctant to release it. He gently used his thumb to caress her palm before turning to walk across the room to a door. The sensation of his thumb on her palm remained even after he entered a room lined by bookcases from floor to ceiling. An ornate desk with leather chairs dominated the space.

Victoria followed Clare up the staircase with an elaborately carved banister to the second floor, where she opened the third door on the right. The bedroom was stunning, with two large windows behind silvery-blue drapery. The striped paper covering the walls was a shade darker, contrasting perfectly with the rich rugs on the floor. Victoria was impressed with the high canopy bed with carved posts of gleaming dark wood covered by a plush cream-colored bedspread. A settee, two chairs, and two tables made up the sitting area. Arranged around the marble fireplace, it was a cozy area for talking or reading. A full-length mirror and a vanity were near the adjacent dressing room.

"Miss Victoria, Emma has been shown to her room for the night and will be here to wake you in the morning. In the meantime, I will help you prepare for bed then take a few minutes to unpack your luggage in your dressing room. If you need anything else, pull the cord beside your bed."

Using the washbasin in her dressing room, Victoria washed the travel dust off and changed into her nightclothes. She was in dreamland as soon as her head hit the pillow.

Rain was misting when Victoria awoke. She guessed the time was already ten o'clock. She pulled the cord, and Emma soon appeared.

"My friend, are you rested after traveling from the mainland? I know I slept soundly," Victoria said.

"I was fatigued when we arrived, but my bed was so

comfortable, and I slept well. Hum—" There seemed to be something else Emma wanted to say, but because Victoria was excited about meeting her father, she did not question her perhaps. After Victoria had eaten and put on a day dress, someone knocked. She opened the door to see Allistair still looking weary.

"Lord John asked to see you now, if at all possible," Allistair said. "When I told him you were here, the joy on his face touched my heart. He was beside himself with gladness."

"I'm pleased to know that, and yes, I am ready to see him. Do you think he'll approve of me?" She knew he heard the uncertainty in her voice.

"Yes, I do. I am sure that any man would be proud of such a lovely daughter," he said.

She tried to let his words reassure her, but she was still worried. Allistair must have sensed her nervousness because he offered his arm to lead Victoria to her father's rooms.

Chapter Nine:
The Truth Revealed

LORD JOHN'S suite of rooms was toward the back of the manor in the west wing. With the curtains closed and only one lamp lighting the room, Victoria's eyes had to adjust to the darkness. She saw a distinguish-looking man sitting in a high-back chair with a blanket on his legs. He had the same shaped nose and chin as her. He also had dimples in his cheeks, as she had. His hair was salt and pepper, and his eyes had faint lines etched around the corners, making him look older than his actual age. Allistair made the introductions then left the room.

"Come closer, my dear," Lord John whispered; his invitation seemed laced with anticipation.

"Lord John," her voice trembled. "Why did you wait until now to bring me home?"

"Victoria, I have waited for this day for such a long

time. I can't believe you are here." Lord John touched her face as if to confirm she was real.

"Allistair told me some details, but I want to know all about you," Victoria said, looking at him through eyelashes lined with teardrops.

"I will tell you everything, but it will take a while. Let me start with the story of how Rebecca and I met. I had finished university at Oxford and decided to enjoy one more day in London before heading home. I was strolling in Hyde Park at the fashionable hour when I saw an attractive lady drop her handkerchief. Gallantly, I tapped her shoulder and said, 'Miss, you dropped this.' Her sweet voice as she thanked me hit my heart like an arrow from a bow," Father laughed.

"She probably noticed you first and dropped the handkerchief on purpose," Victoria added with a wink.

"How intuitive of you, because later, she confessed that she had been watching me for several minutes and wanted to meet me," Father said.

"Her stern-looking companion turned back to see why her charge had stopped. She said, 'Young man, explain yourself.' I sweetly said I was merely returning a dropped handkerchief. That was the beginning of our beautiful love story." Father maintained his hold on Victoria's hand as if he would never let it go this time.

"I introduced myself to the companion, Aunt Freddie, first as was proper, and then I mentioned the close connection my parents had with her family. Aunt Freddie then introduced me to Rebecca Stanford. Since there was a connection, they invited me to join them on their walk. I entertained them with stories of school and life on an island. Aunt Freddie invited me to dinner the next day as we walked back towards the park gates. She added that Rebecca's family had already accepted her invitation earlier that morning. She looked at me and winked."

"Do you know if Aunt Freddie is still alive? I want to meet her. She seems an intriguing character," Victoria said. She selected a chair to sit on and moved as close as possible to Lord John.

"She is, and we correspond often," he replied. "She does not know that you are alive or here on the island. I will have to invite her to come if she is well, and if not, you must go to London to meet her.

"I took my leave and couldn't help softly laughing at Aunt Freddie's matchmaking. I was excited to get to know Rebecca and could not wait to have dinner with them. Entering my rooms, I composed two notes—one to change my departure date and one to my family on DuPree Island. I said I needed a few more days to finish everything before heading home.

"Rebecca and I spent as much time together as possible before I got a message saying I needed to come home as soon as possible. Knowing I might not return to London for a long time, I decided to ask Rebecca to be my wife. She said 'yes,' and we were married within the week by special license."

"Do you have a wedding portrait?" Victoria hoped he did. She wanted to see her mother. She could feel her spirit here with Lord John, but Victoria wanted a firm image of her face in her mind any time she thought of her.

Lord John asked her to move the curtain on the wall across from his bed. Victoria could only gasp with excitement, which quickly turned to despair when she saw the painting of her mother and father in their wedding attire. The artist had captured her parents' passion and love. Victoria was sad, knowing she would never know her mother. She leaned down and hugged her father again before retaking her seat.

"It's an enchanting portrait," she whispered.

"Your mother was so captivating, and I miss her every day."

She gripped his hand until he was composed. "Lord John, are you sure you want to continue now?"

"Victoria, I don't want another minute to go by without you knowing that everything we did was for you. Now, where did I leave off? Let me explain why we left you on the doorstep; I guess I should start before you were born. This is hard to admit, but you need to know this part first." Father seemed to be torn about what he had to say next.

"My mother—your grandmother, Esther—had a baby girl seven years after I was born. Her name was Karen. I was excited about having a baby sister. My father, whose name was William, was delighted. But Esther was distant and didn't seem to have the energy to even nurse Karen. Many times, the nanny had to remind her to feed the baby.

"Victoria, this part was one of the most traumatic times of my life. Allistair knows, but I asked him to let me tell you," Lord John continued. "I wish I didn't have to share this with you, but I must explain why your mother and I were afraid for your life. A week after Karen was born, my father had to go to the mainland on business. I was in my room at the time, looking out a window facing the waves. I hoped to see my father's ship returning. If the winds were in his favor, he should be back any minute, I knew.

"Something caught my eye; I saw my mother walking towards the sea. I thought she was outside to wait for Father's return. I did wonder why she was getting so close to the edge of the cliff. What happened next, I will never forget. Burned into my memory forever, I saw my mother raise her arms overhead and throw a wiggling baby, Karen, into the sea."

Paralyzed by disbelief, Victoria couldn't say a word. Lord John seemed to be looking back in time and kept telling her what he had witnessed that day.

"I ran as fast as I could towards the hilltop where my mother stood. I carefully approached the edge to see if there was any chance Karen was still alive. I knew how hopeless the situation was when I saw Karen's blanket sink beneath the waves. Esther reached for me, but I dodged her outstretched hands and ran as far away as possible. Later, Father found me in the stables. He held me close as we tried to console one another."

"Oh, you must have been traumatized," Victoria cried.

"Very much so. Our family was not the same after that. When I was older, I found out my father almost killed Esther with his bare hands that day. He would have succeeded if Allistair's father, Paul, had not stopped him."

Lord John reached a trembling hand to cover his eyes as though trying to block the visions in his head. "My father moved all his belongings to a suite of rooms as far away from Esther as possible. He refused to even dine with her in the dining room. He either ate in his rooms or waited for Esther to finish first. Until then, we had been a perfect family. I never understood why Esther, my own mother, did what she did. Something must have been wrong with her mentally. Emotionally, I was distant from her, though I saw her every day and sometimes even had dinner with her, usually once a week."

Father stopped for a couple of minutes. He lifted his eyes, and Victoria saw the sorrow he couldn't put into words.

"I told your mother that my parents were estranged and lived separately in the manor, but I didn't give any details. Esther was nice to your mother and seemed glad I had found a wonderful woman for my wife. When we found out we were having you, your grandmother helped prepare the nursery and talked about having a grandson. But all that changed when you were born. When the midwife brought you out to show the family and said to me, 'It's a girl!' I was enchanted by you.

"I turned to show you to Esther, and for a second, I thought I saw a strange look on her face that I didn't understand. Maybe I was mistaken because when I blinked, she touched your tiny hand and cooed over you.

"Rebecca kept you close during the first couple of

months of your life. She preferred you to stay in our rooms so she could nurse you as needed. When you were five months old, Esther asked to take you outside for some fresh air. Rebecca needed a break, and since Esther had been so loving during the months after you were born, she agreed. Rebecca had no reason to worry since she didn't know the whole story of how my sister had died."

Victoria cried out and covered her face with her hands. "I think I will be sick if—"

She looked up at Lord John, who nodded his head to confirm her worst fear. "Many times, over the years, I have wished I had told your mother about my sister's death. Maybe if I had, then what happened next would not have transpired," he said, with much regret.

"My father was away from the manor, checking on the new crops, but thank goodness I decided to work on the books and not accompany him. Rebecca found me in the study and asked if I wanted to take a walk with her on the beach. I was so pleased to be alone with her I did not ask who was watching the baby. We held hands and had a wonderful time enjoying being together."

"Father, I'm afraid for you to continue the story. Did my own grandmother try to kill me?" Victoria was visibly trembling.

"Esther quickly gathered you up and left the manor. She took the path to the same hilltop where she threw Karen into the sea. As she neared the cliff, I saw her and knew she meant to do the same to you. I climbed the hill from the beach as fast as possible. I was determined to save you and was behind Esther within a couple of minutes.

She heard me coming and turned her head towards me, looking demented. I tried to reason with her as I inched closer. With her back to me, she seemed to shake herself out of a trance and asked, 'Why am I here?' As she appeared to be raising her arms to throw you, I grabbed her and pulled you from her grip.

"Esther crumbled to the ground and wept. She kept saying, 'I don't know why I am here,' as the butler and farm foreman helped her back to the manor.

"A servant was sent to find my father. We knew we had to do something so she could never harm anyone ever again. We agreed to hire a companion who would also be her keeper. The first one to take on this responsibility started spreading rumors that Esther was oppressed by the spirit of a witch who lived on the island many years ago. This witch allegedly sacrificed baby girls to the sea gods to ensure they provided pleasant weather, a great bounty of fish, and abundant harvests. When my father found out, he released her from her duty. He tried to stop the 'whispers' about Esther, but some still believe. Some on the island still claim they see the gods on the sea's horizon at certain times of the year, waiting for another sacrifice.

"The next keeper was a spinster lady named Suzie. She has been with Esther ever since. Allistair's mother, Martha, takes over when Suzie has a day off. Esther is now confined to her rooms in the tower.

"Later, when Rebecca was calmer, I told her the whole story of my sister's death and apologized for not doing so beforehand. I told her why my father didn't divorce Esther or send her away after throwing Karen in the sea," said

Lord John, with a hollowness of despair in his voice.

Victoria swallowed her hurt and lifted her chin defiantly. "I'm trying to understand. You kept a killer here on the island but left me on a doorstep in London. Why wasn't Esther declared insane? Surely, she could have been put in a private home on the mainland where she could never hurt anyone ever again," said Victoria. The ferocity of her own voice surprised her.

"Victoria, I know it seems we valued Esther over you, but there is a reason. What I am going to tell you must remain between you and me. No one else knows the reason, not even Esther.

"When my father received a Barony and this island for services rendered to Queen Victoria, it didn't come with any money. He knew he had to marry a titled lady of wealth to make this island a productive place. He also had to convince workers to move their families to the island, but he had to clear the land and build homes for them first. Everything he needed required money. So, he made the rounds of social events in London where he met Lady Esther Spellington during her coming-out ball. Her father was Duke of Spell and was extremely rich. Lady Esther had many suitors, but she fell in love with Lord William. The Duke of Spell didn't want anyone to marry Lady Esther for her money, so in the wedding contract, he put in two stipulations: she could never be divorced nor put in a mental asylum, which is sadly common when some men tire of their wives."

"Surely the contract could have been broken," Victoria said, with a deep aching need to know why she had to miss getting to know her mother while Esther still got to live on the island. She glared at him without blinking.

"My father tried to break the contract both times to no avail. I even testified as a witness to her deeds. We tried, but the court announced that the contract was incontestable and not changeable."

"Father, I am stunned by what you have told me, but I now understand why you had to leave me in London. I feel for everyone, including Grandmother. One of my charitable endeavors in London was setting up a home for ladies who have mental disorders. I am glad that many doctors now recognize most symptoms of mental imbalance are real instead of 'female hysterics' or 'devil possessions' as once thought."

"When you were ten months old," Lord John continued, "we decided things were too dangerous for you to live on the island. I wanted to move to London with you and your mother, but money was tight after two brutal winters resulted in reduced crop yields. After many sleepless nights and rejecting plan after plan, we finally settled on one that would keep you safe. This plan, unfortunately, meant separation from you. We hoped it wouldn't last for terribly long.

"I used the excuse that I was looking for potential financial opportunities and that I needed to present you to Rebecca's family as the reasons we decided to travel to London. Unknown to those on the island, we decided to leave you with some friends of your mother's older brother. We didn't want anything to lead back to us or the island, so we stayed in a hotel near the river, far from the Montgomerys' townhome."

Father stopped to drink water, and Victoria could feel his heartbreak over that decision.

"Earlier in the day, I was hiding in the shrubs near the Montgomerys' servants' entrance and heard the cook talking about Lady Montgomery attending the opera that night, which meant she didn't have to cook for a group.

"We knew this would be the best time to leave you, so we prepared a basket, wrapped you in a blanket made of the finest material, and included a note and a silver rattle. Since the message was on quality paper, and the handwriting pointed to a highly educated person, we believed the Montgomerys would know that somebody from a prominent family had left the child. The note asked them to raise the infant as their own, and because of a threat made to harm our baby, we could not keep her."

"Hannah Montgomery kept everything, including the basket you left me in," said Victoria. "They agreed to wait until my twenty-first birthday to tell me everything and give me those items. Because I could see and touch the basket and everything else, I knew they were telling the truth. I'm glad I will always have these treasures."

"Victoria, I'm pleased you have them. Your mother cried over each object as she placed them in the basket. That night, I quickly left you on the front steps of their townhome. Rebecca and I hid nearby to make sure somebody would take you in. We saw Lady Montgomery walk up the steps just as you started to cry. She gathered you close and went inside the townhome."

"Your hearts must have been ripped out." Tears ran fresh from Victoria's eyes as she thought of them having to leave her.

Taking several deep breaths, Lord John adjusted the blanket around himself and continued. "Your mother reached out as if to get you, then almost fainted when the doors closed. The hardest thing I've ever done was not breaking down those doors and taking you home. Around midnight, I finally convinced your mother to return to the hotel. We discussed the next part of our plan until dawn, when she finally declared we had to finish everything we had started. She kissed me, then closed her eyes, and sank into a deep, exhausted slumber, as I recall.

"The next part of our plan was to make sure you were not put in an orphanage. I dressed in a servant's uniform, returned to the Montgomerys, and posed as somebody looking for a new job.

"As you know, servants talk about everything going on in the household. I hoped I would find out something about you. I went to the servants' entrance to inquire about a job, and luck was with me as they needed somebody to fill a vacant position. While meeting with the butler, I overhead the others talking about the Montgomerys trying to find the baby's parents. They also heard them talking about adopting the baby. With no leads, they hired a private detective to find out anything he could."

"A private detective? Were you scared he would find you?" Victoria wondered.

"Yes, I was afraid. The butler believed my made-up

story and asked when I could start. I said I needed to get my possessions and would come back later that day.

"When I heard that a private detective was looking for your mother and me, I hurried back to the hotel, knowing we needed to leave. I hired a carriage, and we left town within the hour. To keep the detective off our trail, I asked a porter to book us two tickets to Madagascar, knowing there was no way they could check all the stops the ship would make. We traveled to Cardiff, Wales, so I could meet a potential wheat buyer. That was our 'cover story' when we decided we needed to leave you in London for your safety.

"As soon as we arrived at the docks in Cardiff for the trip to the island, a message reached us that Allistair's father, Paul, was dead from a farming accident. The responsibility for Paul's family was now mine. Allistair was only five, and his mother was now a widow.

"When we arrived back at the manor, we told everyone that you died from a fever on the return trip and that you were buried at sea. Your mother was so depressed because of the decision to leave you in London that she didn't have to act upset about your 'death.' Everyone was so loving towards us, which helped with the grieving process."

The clock struck the half-hour. Lord John reached for a small bowl beside the chair and removed several small white tablets. He took them with a few messy sips of water.

"I promised your mother that I would bring you home as soon as possible. We did not have much contact with Esther over the years and did not notice she was losing weight until Suzie, against Esther's wishes, told us one night after dinner. A doctor from the mainland diagnosed her as having leukemia. Not much was known about it back then, including life expectancy. The doctor said he thought she would only live three years at the most. I could only look at that as a blessing and that we would be able to bring you home soon. But Esther was stubborn and is still alive. Some on the island say the sea keeps her alive—superstitious nonsense.

"Victoria, your mother passed away two years after you were left on the doorstep. She died giving birth to your brother, Daniel. Right now, Daniel is on his way home from university. I have not told him you are alive. In the note to him about coming home, he was told to come to me as soon as he gets here because I have important news to tell him."

"I'm excited about having a brother. I grew up an only child and was lonely until my companion, Emma, joined the household. She and I are as close as sisters. I'll bring her to meet you later in the week," Victoria said, letting her father know she looked forward to building a relationship with Daniel and hoped he would like Emma, too.

"I know this must be a surprise for you to discover your birth family after all this time, but please try to understand we knew of no other way to keep you safe. When your mother passed away, I thought I would bring you home, but you had already bonded with the Montgomerys. I couldn't justify tearing a five-year-old away from everything she knew. I'm sure you have wondered why I kept Daniel with me. The first year of his life, I felt so alone without your mother. I put all my energy into raising him and dealing with many problems here on the island."

"Oh, I do understand. I wish I could have known my mother, however," Victoria said, with a healing warmth traveling through her body.

"Your mother knew that one day I would be able to bring you home, so she wrote you a letter and made me promise, as soon as you arrived, to give it to you. I told her don't be silly because she would be here when you returned. She gave me a bittersweet smile as if she knew otherwise."

Lord John reached under the quilt over his legs, then handed Victoria a letter, which had turn browned around the edges with age. "I'm exhausted. Would you mind if we talk later this afternoon? The doctor said I do not have much longer to live, but please do not worry about me. I shall die happy knowing that I was able to bring my sweet daughter home."

"Please don't talk about dying. We shall make the best of the time we have together. Let me ring for your manservant," she said, before rising to leave. As she closed the door to her father's rooms, she saw Allistair near the end of the hall.

"Hello, is everything all right? Do you want to talk about anything now?"

"Allistair, would you please walk me back to my rooms? I have much to think about, and Father gave me a letter from my mother that I need to read before I meet more of the family."

"Yes," he said. "Would you like lunch sent to your rooms, or would you rather eat with my mother and me? Oh, I am sorry I forgot to tell you that my mother lives here, too. My father died when I was only five."

"Father told me about his accident. I'm sorry. Yes, thank you. Lunch with you both would be great. I look forward to meeting your mother. I am sure that she and I will be great friends."

After Allistair left her at her bedroom door, Victoria settled in a comfortable chair and opened the letter.

My darling, Victoria,

Your brother or sister is due soon. I am excited but scared, too. I have had a strong feeling that I should write this letter to you. I must put on paper how much I love you and wish you were here with us.

Long before you entered this world, your father and I knew you would be the manifestation of our love. I understood love so completely the day you were born and placed in my arms. Your father and I could only look at you with wonder that together we had made such a sweet baby. Every time you rested your tiny head on my chest, my heart melted. Looking at you, I realized how innocent you were and wanted to make sure you were always safe.

I was thrilled to watch you start to grow and change before my eyes. I tried to imagine you in each stage until you became a grown woman and started your own family.

The day we almost lost you will be on my mind forever. Your father saved you; try not to think about what could have happened. I became overly protective of you, and only your father could pick you up. You had just started teething and trying to crawl. Allistair played with you and encouraged you to crawl to him. The day you did, we all clapped. I was so delighted but also worried that something would happen to you. I could not rest at night, thinking somebody would take you from me.

I thought that was the worst day of my life but leaving you in London left a hole in my heart only your return could fill. It wasn't easy for me to dress or venture out of my bedroom. Knowing we could not bring you home while Esther was alive made me wish for her death. I know I should not think that way, but I cannot help myself. I have nightmares often that Esther could easily get out of the tower.

Two years after we left you on a doorstep, I found out I was going to have another baby. I was terrified. What if Esther tried to kill him or her? Your father was such a patient, loving man, and he eventually coaxed me out for walks on the beach and dinner in the dining room.

Your father makes me feel that I am the most charming and strongest woman ever. He is the kindest, most loyal man I know. On the day you were born, and he held you in his arms, I knew he would always be your champion and take care of you. After carefully looking at every choice, the pain was almost more than we could handle when we had to leave you in London. Please know this is the truth; it was not an easy decision for us to make.

As you grow, I hope you know that life will bring new adventures and surprises your way. Be brave as you face them. I want you to explore new opportunities, challenge yourself – do not always take the safe choice, try new things, and always give your best in all you do. Do not let the fear of failure or others' judgment of you stop you from doing everything you know you should.

Always offer a kind word or simple gesture to those not as privileged as you.

I hope we can be together soon.
With all my love,
Mother

While reading the letter, Victoria was unaware that tears flowed down her face until she saw the wet marks on her dress. She would never fully know her mother and never be able to sit and talk to her.

Someone knocked on the door. She thought it was Allistair and said, "Come in."

"Hello, Victoria, I am Martha DuPree, Allistair's mother," said a nice-looking woman with graying hair and sparkling green eyes.

"How do you do? I am glad to meet you," Victoria said, brushing the remaining tears from her cheeks.

"Please excuse me if I am intruding," Martha said, when she noticed the letter lying in Victoria's lap and her red eyes. "Allistair said you would join us for lunch, so I have come to show you the way to the dining room. You can get lost until you learn your way around this big old house."

"That is so nice of you. Let me wash my face, and I'll be ready to go with you."

In a few minutes, they made their way to the dining room and chatted about small, unimportant things such as the weather on the island. Victoria was glad that Martha had not asked her any personal questions. She was afraid if they talked about serious things, she would start to cry again.

The dining room was magnificent. The massive oak table, covered with a white silk tablecloth, could seat at least fifty people when extended. Portraits of the DuPree ancestry covered the richly paneled walls. Victoria noticed all the men had the same cerulean-blue eyes as Lord John and Allistair. A sizable carved fireplace was located at the far side of the room. She noticed that the table was not set for lunch. Before she could make an inquiry, Martha led her to the massive doors leading outside.

"When your mother moved in, she created this area to take advantage of the view while having a more intimate place to dine. She enjoyed being outside."

The view down to the shore took away Victoria's breath; it was such a stunning place. She had just read the letter from her mother, so Rebecca's presence seemed to be in every flower and shrub. The dining setup was more casual here, and the pretty floral-cushioned chairs looked so comfortable. There were three place settings, and Martha asked her to take the one with the best view overlooking the sea.

"Excuse my lateness," Allistair said, coming around the corner of the home. He bowed to Victoria and took a seat to her left. "Victoria, if the weather is good, we usually have lunch out here. Dinner will be in the dining room and will be much more elaborate. Your father usually has breakfast and lunch in his rooms but will come down for dinner.

"I do believe that Lord John looks much better. I am glad to see some color in his face. His last attack was serious. We thought he would not make it, but he seemed to improve at once when he heard I had brought you to see him. Again, I want to thank you for coming."

Martha and Victoria talked about the latest fashions, their opinions of motor-driven vehicles, and innovative ideas and inventions now available. Martha said she had not been to London in years. Victoria could see the sadness in her eyes and thought she must be remembering her husband.

Victoria found Martha to be nice, but there was a mysteriousness about her. Was she hiding something? Victoria wondered if the mystery had something to do with Esther. She remembered her father said Martha was her "keeper" when the companion had a day off.

Chapter Ten:
First Lovers' Kiss

VICTORIA, do you want to ride with me for a tour of the island? Now is the perfect moment since Lord John usually takes a nap around this time every day," Allistair said, rising from the table after they had a stimulating lunch. She agreed and went to change into her riding habit. Victoria felt relief not having to worry about Father asking for her while they were out riding. She checked to make sure he was comfortable before going back downstairs. He looked so peaceful lying upon his bed. She bent over and lightly kissed his cheek.

In a few minutes, Allistair and Victoria were headed to the stables. As they walked toward a building that could house at least twenty horses, she got a good look at the manor and surrounding gardens. The manor, constructed of bricks mellowed with age to a rosy color, had long gracious windows. The front veranda, supported by four sculptured columns, rose to the second floor. Rose vines entwined each column. Victoria could hardly wait for spring to see their colors. She did not ask Allistair what color the roses would be; she wanted to be surprised. The immaculate gardens looked well-tended with each blade of grass in its place. The scent from the flowers and shrubs would soon fill the air. There were stone statues and benches placed throughout.

Victoria could see several horses already being exercised in the paddocks after they arrived at the stables. Allistair walked all the way to the back stall.

"A surprise is waiting for you in here." He called for Victoria to come to the back.

When she looked in the stall, she saw the Arabian stallion her parents had given her for her birthday.

"How did my horse get here?" She gently touched its muzzle.

"Early this morning, a groom delivered your horse. He said they had a good trip with no mishaps." Allistair opened the stall door.

Victoria unhooked the bridle and led him from the stall. Someone had already saddled the stallion, so he was ready for their ride.

"Have you given him a name?" Allistair asked as he walked with her into the bright sunshine, where she saw a second horse waiting for him to ride.

"I haven't had time to give him a name. I was so excited about my birthday celebration and preparing for the ball that I completely forgot about him. Since he has a star on his forehead, I think he should be called Star."

Victoria felt a sense of pride that DuPree Island was her heritage when she saw how diverse the terrain was with beaches, valleys, and mountains. As they rode at a fast clip, they bypassed the farms, villagers' homes, the doctor's office, and the two local storehouses.

Allistair took off at a trot, and Victoria followed. He slowed his horse and turned to her with a charming grin.

"Victoria, you allowed me to see your special place on the mainland, and now I want to show you my special place on the island. I found solace here when my father died. If I am having a distressing day, if possible, I come here, and all the tension is released."

Dismounting, they climbed a low hill and came upon a multi-tiered waterfall over sixty feet high, surrounded by a lovely, wooded area. The stream split into four segments before coming together again near the bottom, giving it a diamond shape. Allistair took her closer to the pool at the bottom. She could see herself swimming there in the summer. The pool emptied into a small river that flowed down the other side of the hill.

Allistair took her hand and led her up to the top. The going was challenging in several places. Once her feet came out from beneath her as she tried to gain a foothold, but Allistair helped her before she could fall. When they reached the top, and after encouragement from Allistair, Victoria sat down, removed her shoes, and put her feet in the refreshing water. The coldness took her breath away. Laughing, she looked up to find Allistair was behind her. She turned her face toward him. He gently bent over, placed a hand on her shoulder, and kissed her cheek.

Before Victoria could stop herself, she grabbed his hand, pulling him down beside her. They sat for several seconds, staring into each other's eyes. Allistair uttered a strange sound before jumping to his feet. Victoria's hopes dropped, and she thought she had done something wrong. But just as fast, he pulled her to her feet. Since he was over six feet tall, she did not come up to his shoulders. Victoria guessed he could see the desire in her eyes because he pulled her closer to his lean, hard body, and his mouth descended to hers. This was her first lovers' kiss, and she lost all sense of time as his lips gently touched hers. She had never experienced such a wonderful feeling. Reluctantly, he let her go.

"Victoria. You looked so beautiful, and I could not help myself," Allistair said with a strained voice.

She gave him a hug to let him know that she enjoyed the kiss.

"Let's head home," he said.

They hardly spoke on the ride back. Caught up in her own thoughts, Victoria was afraid to break the magical spell. Allistair helped her dismount and held her hand for a few more seconds than necessary.

"I'm glad you agreed to go riding with me," Allistair whispered. Laughing, Victoria ran ahead and entered the side door.

Once in the manor, she went to her rooms to change for dinner. She decided she would surprise her father by wearing the dress he had designed for her. Victoria was ready a half-hour before the dinner gong, so she went to his rooms.

"Father, do you like the gown you gave me for my birthday?" She twirled around to show him the whole dress.

"My dear, I knew you would look angelic in it."

They talked for several minutes, then there was a knock on the door. Allistair entered. "Lord John, I have come to help you to the dining room." As Father turned to retrieve his walking stick, Victoria looked up to see the glow on Allistair's face. He winked at her, and she felt a much too revealing blush come to her cheeks. Father looked from her to Allistair but did not say a word.

The food at dinner, which included items grown locally, and the wine were superb.

"Did you enjoy your first ride around the island?" Father asked.

"Yes, I did," answered Victoria. "Everything is so unusual but impressive, especially the waterfall."

She could not help glancing at Allistair when she said that part. She saw he was ogling her, so he did not notice the deep frown on his mother's face. Victoria wondered what had caused Martha's reaction.

"Allistair always goes to the waterfall when he needs to think or get away from everything," said Martha, with a slight pinch in her lips. "You, however, are the first person he has taken there." She quickly looked around the room and motioned to the butler. "Higgins, please serve brandy and coffee in the drawing room."

Victoria noticed Father looked tired, so she excused herself to help him to his rooms.

"Here, let me assist you," said Allistair.

"If you don't mind, I want to spend a few more minutes with Father before he goes to sleep. I will meet you and Martha for coffee soon."

Minutes later, Victoria entered the drawing room and accepted a cup from Martha. She slowly drank her coffee as she listened to Allistair and his mother discuss the activities planned for the week. Feeling a bit ignored, Victoria put down the cup and told them goodnight. As she reached the bedroom door, she heard footsteps behind her.

Allistair was walking toward her. "Victoria, do you need to talk about anything?"

"No, Allistair; I want to go to bed early tonight," she said with a yawn.

"I hope you have sweet dreams," he said. "Tomorrow, I can show you the business side of the island if you wish. How would you like to go on a picnic? We could go to the grounds around the lighthouse. Do you want to invite Emma and my mother?"

"Allistair, yes to all you suggested." She could not resist touching his cheek before she entered her rooms. He grabbed her hand and placed a kiss on her upturned palm before bowing and walking away.

She entered her rooms, holding the hand he had kissed to her heart. She could see herself falling deeper into the blue sea in Allistair's eyes. She knew she was falling in love with him. But she cautioned herself to keep that knowledge a secret. With everything going on, she needed to make sure she wasn't looking for a lifeline should her entire world fall from under her feet.

Victoria began an emotional letter to her Montgomery parents. She informed them what she had just learned about the DuPrees. She decided to write each day then send the letter at the end of the week. Victoria found that if she wrote everything down, she could better understand and share the revelations with her other family.

Victoria thought she would reminisce for a long time, but she was out as soon as her head touched the pillow.

Victoria was standing at the top of the waterfall, but Allistair was not there. She was afraid and could not move. Somebody was coming up behind her to push her down to the pool below. She could not turn her head to see who the assailant was nor cry out for help. She was frozen, but the fear was so real, she felt perspiration between her breasts and on her forehead. Just as the cold hands pressed against her back, ready to push her . . . .

Victoria awoke with a half scream. For a minute, she didn't know where she was and could only see the foot of the bed bathed in the light of the moon from the open window.

Was her subconscious warning her to be cautious? These people were strangers, after all. Did somebody think she was an interloper?

Chapter Eleven:
Picnic at the Lighthouse

THE NEXT day, Victoria selected a pretty day dress for the picnic. She looked forward to seeing the lighthouse since she had never been in one before. She could only imagine the view for miles from the top gallery.

Everyone agreed it was one of those rare, perfect days for a picnic. A thirty-minute stroll along a gravel path brought them to the grassy hill where the octagonal lighthouse stood sentinel over the turbulent sea below.

"The lighthouse is constructed of stone quarried here on the island and rises to a height of over eighty feet," Allistair explained, along with how it emits light from a system of lamps and lenses.

"We have a full-time lighthouse keeper who lives in it and makes sure the lamps never go out. The light has saved many mariners from shipwreck on the island and the submerged rocks offshore," Allistair said, helping the ladies step over a fallen log. "Since sea fogs can engulf the island quickly, a bell is sounded from the lighthouse once every five seconds. The first time you hear the fog bell can be eerie."

The cook provided baskets with more food than they could eat. For lunch, they had their pick of roasted chicken, slices of ham, a green salad, fruit turnovers, a few jam puffs, rolls, a tin of mixed biscuits, lemonade, and wine. Everything they needed was in the baskets, including plates, glasses, and utensils.

Allistair spread blankets under the shade of the towering trees surrounding the grassy hill. They enjoyed the food and friendly conversation with the sea breezes blowing softly and the sun-dappled tree canopy overhead. Laughter echoed down to the beach.

After lunch, everyone walked up the hill to tour the lighthouse. The light-keeper was enthusiastic as well as serious about keeping islanders and sea vessels safe.

"… Only I can go in the lantern room because the lenses need to be spotless at all times. We will, however, see the watch room that, to me, is spectacular. It is outfitted with windows through which you can observe water conditions during storms," he informed everyone.

"Living here my whole life, I have never been on a tour of the lighthouse, I'm sorry to say," declared Martha. "This will be so exciting." She and Emma followed the light-keeper.

At the top of the stairs, Allistair opened the door to the gallery circling the top floor. "Are you afraid of heights," he asked Victoria.

"No. I actually like being high and looking down below," Victoria said, as Allistair took her hand, and they stepped out. Victoria marveled at the sight before her. She realized how large and beautiful the island was seeing it from this vantage point. She half-listened to the light-keeper explain the workings of the lighthouse. Mesmerized by the view, she walked to the other side of the gallery. From there, she could see most of the island, including the village.

Victoria drew closer to the railing and looked down. She quickly moved as far back as the tower wall would allow, squeezing her eyes shut with fear so intense, she could hardly breathe. A few seconds later, Victoria knew she needed to confirm what she had seen. She stepped closer to the railing once again and looked down. Sure enough, the man from her birthday ball and the coaching inn was on DuPree Island. He was staring at her and gave her a half-wave before turning to walk through the trees.

Chapter Twelve: Who is the Spy?

WHEN VICTORIA entered the breakfast room, she was surprised to hear Father laughing at something Allistair said. She could feel her whole face light up with joy. "Father, I'm so glad you are joining us for breakfast this morning. Hearing you laugh is so uplifting."

"Victoria, I feel wonderful, but I won't do more than I should. Allistair was telling a story about the new foal born this morning. I have seen many foals taking their first steps over the years. I am always thrilled to see new life. And having you back has given me new life as well."

After they finished breakfast, Victoria accompanied Father back to his rooms. He said he had something he needed to tell her. After all she had already heard, she felt she was mentally prepared to face anything.

As they sat together on his settee, he took her hand.

"I wanted to know about your life in London, so I planted someone in the Montgomery household who could give me reports."

"I don't understand. You 'planted' someone? You mean a *spy*?"

"I sent a letter to the Stanfords about someone I knew who needed a job. I asked if they could help secure this person a position. I had heard the Montgomerys were looking for a companion for their daughter. I hinted to the Stanfords that they could recommend my person for that position." Father stopped to let Victoria figure out about whom he was talking.

"Emma?" Victoria guessed, with a look of disbelief.

"Yes, Emma. She did not know about you being my daughter, however. She was my housekeeper's daughter. As a child, Emma and Allistair played together a lot since she was here most days with her mother. They shared a tutor because they were the same age, and I believe girls should receive the same education as boys. The tutor reported that she was an excellent student, and he hoped she would find a great position as a companion in a prestigious English home. When her mother passed away, I decided to send her to Mrs. Hilbert's Finishing School to give her the skills needed for a great position. That is when the idea to get her in the Montgomery household came to me. Named the student 'Most Likely to Succeed' upon completing her studies, I told her I would help her secure a position with one of my family's friends.

"Everything fell into place. The Stanfords told the Montgomerys about Emma. Since neither family knew you were my daughter, they thought they had the best recommendation for someone to fill the position. I promise you: Emma knew nothing other than that I had recommended her for the position. I was glad that you two became so close. Please don't be angry at her."

"Now that I think about it, Emma has been acting strange lately. Several times she seemed to want to tell me something. As soon as she met Allistair at the Montgomerys' home, her expression of surprise seemed odd," Victoria said, stunned by this revelation.

"I asked Emma to send me a detailed monthly letter of everything she did in London and what life was like living with the Montgomery family," said Father. "I wanted to know if she was progressing well in her new employment. Since Emma was your companion, I asked about your time together and if you were a good person who cared about her and the other staff. She filled her letters with more details than I could have hoped. They gave me a great picture of her life with you. I told her to keep her personal life here on the island to herself and only talk about being in the finishing school when asked about herself.

"I supplemented her salary as a way of helping her family. Her brother, Henry, joined the Royal Navy, leaving their father alone on the island.

"Before I came down to breakfast this morning, I asked Emma to come see me. I explained everything to her. Instead of being upset that I had asked her to spy on you, the dear woman said she was glad she had the opportunity to help me connect with you when I could not bring you home."

"Father, you had no other way of making sure I was contented living with the Montgomerys. I will talk to Emma this morning and let her know I appreciate all that she has done. She is my best friend, and that is all because you were concerned for my wellbeing."

In her bedroom, Victoria rang for Emma. They discussed everything, and both said they understood Lord John's reasons for sending Emma to be Victoria's companion.

"Emma, I am glad you are my friend and want you to continue as my companion. But, if you decide to move back to London and take another position, I will be glad to give you a wonderful referral." Victoria crossed her fingers behind her back that she would choose to stay with her.

"The island is my home, and I would be honored to continue as your companion." Emma smiled. "Would you like to meet my father? He lives a few miles away. We could ride horses, and I can show you the village where most fieldworker families live. We can go after lunch if you would like," Emma said.

"That is a good idea. I look forward to meeting your father and learning about your childhood," Victoria replied.

Chapter Thirteen: An Open Grave Awaits

AFTER LUNCH, Victoria and Emma changed and met at the stables. Their ride to the village showed how the DuPree family took great care of their workers. The islanders were able to buy their own homes, which most had already done. Many of the houses were immaculately kept.

"Homes needing to be fixed are owned by widows or those with sickness in the family," Emma disclosed.

Victoria had already been thinking of ways the DuPree family could help the islanders. She was waiting for the right time to present her plan to her father.

Emma's father, Simon Jonas, was a hospitable man. His love for Emma was plain to see.

"Miss Victoria, thank you for being so good to my Emma," said Mr. Jonas. "My girl told me you two are as close as sisters."

Emma showed Victoria some of her favorite places in and near the village. They returned to have tea with Mr. Jonas. He asked Emma if she could help him with something that would only take thirty minutes.

"I want to ride back to the manor by myself. I know the way and will be fine. You spend as much time with your father as you want. I'll see you later," Victoria said, thanking Mr. Jonas for his hospitality.

Ten minutes into her ride, Victoria noticed fog quickly rolling toward her, obscuring everything more than an arm's length away. Disoriented, Victoria dismounted and led her horse while she tried to figure out where she was.

When she finally saw the island cemetery in front of her, an eerie bell sounded, making her jump. Star was unfamiliar with the fog, so he became spooked when the bell rang and pulled his reins from Victoria's hand. Before she could stop him, Star was gone, a fading thumping of hooves vanishing in the fog.

Victoria had only seen the cemetery from afar while riding with Allistair. Since she didn't trust walking in an open field, not knowing what accident could happen to her, she decided to look for her mother's gravesite.

When she opened the weather-worn iron gate, chills traveled down her spine as it creaked like a door without oil. With the fog surrounding her in a thick heavy mist, she followed the path as it began winding through the spooky graveyard. Ancient, engraved tombstones guided the way. Normal everyday noises, such as branches creaking, sounded strange and creepy to her ears as dark shadows surrounded her. Her heart began to beat faster. The air smelled of damp earth, and rotten dead leaves accumulated around the mist-shrouded tombstones and underneath the low-hanging tree limbs. Her footsteps squished with each step she took through slimy brown mud. She almost fell but caught herself in time. She looked to her left and saw the tombstone for her mother, Rebecca.

Victoria used her boot to wipe dead leaves off the grave marker. She would have sat down to talk to her mother if the ground weren't wet from rain that had fallen overnight. She bent over instead.

"Mother, I wish you were here. I didn't even know about you until a few days ago, but I can feel you close. I understand why you and Lord John left me in London, but I can't help wondering what my life would have been with you in it. Your letter was beautiful, and I could sense your presence as I read it.

"I think I'm falling in love with Allistair. I need your guidance to make sure it's love and not just needing someone to help me feel more anchored to this world. Mother, I love you," she said, wiping away tears she didn't even know were running down her cheeks until now. But that wasn't all Victoria noticed.

The fog obscured the sun.

The birds had fallen silent.

The wind didn't blow.

All was still, too still, until Victoria heard footsteps slowly coming toward her. Straightening, she decided to start walking forward.

"Hello, who's there?" she called out to see if it were someone looking for her.

No one answered, but the footsteps continued.

Victoria carefully moved through mud and broken tombstones before stopping and listening, but she didn't hear the footsteps anymore. Was she mistaken? She began looking at the headstones again. She noticed one with fresh flowers in the urn and bent over to have a closer look. The engraving on the stone read *Paul DuPree*. She had found Allistair's father's grave. Martha must have been there within the last couple of days. Heartbreak was still Martha's friend.

Somebody grabbed Victoria from behind. Before she could scream, a gloved hand clamped over her mouth. A man with hot sour breath lifted her so that her feet didn't touch the ground. He quickly carried her to an open grave, put her down long enough to hit her over the head, then threw her in the freshly dug hole.

"Emma, did you and Victoria enjoy your visit with your

father?" Allistair asked her, when he passed her in the hallway on his way to the drawing room. He realized he had not seen Victoria since lunch.

"Yes, it was a good visit. After tea, Victoria decided to ride back by herself. She said she knew the way. I stayed to help my dad and then had to wait for the fog to dissipate. She should be down for dinner soon. I am headed to her rooms to help her get ready," Emma answered.

Within minutes, Emma rushed into the drawing room.

"Allistair, when I went to Victoria's rooms, there wasn't any sign that she had been there at all. Her riding habit wasn't in the dressing room. I asked the staff, but no one has seen her since lunch. I'm worried. Maybe the fog confused her, and she lost her way."

Allistair quickly rose and went to the stables and found she had not returned her horse. He and several stable hands checked outside to see if the horse had returned without her. Located near the stables, Star was unharmed, but there wasn't any sign of Victoria.

With the fog still hanging over the island, a search party began to look for her. They spread out, heading toward the Jonas' home. Nearing the graveyard, they noticed the gate was open. They went inside to search and heard a voice screaming "Help."

Allistair motioned for everyone to stop. He could no longer hear the screams. What if they were too late? He couldn't let his mind go there. Since he hadn't been to the graveyard in many years and wasn't familiar with its layout, he didn't know which way to search first. He sent some of the men to the east side while he led a group to the west. When Allistair heard someone yell that Victoria was found, he ran, dodging gravestones and sloshing mud everywhere, toward a lantern, which waved in the distant fog. He had to see her for himself. What would Allistair do if Victoria were dead? When he saw men surrounding an open gravesite, he knew that his anguish must have been evident for all to see, but he didn't care. Falling to his knees at the edge of the open grave, Allistair was too afraid to look inside. He couldn't imagine life without his one true love. When he saw Victoria sitting up and looking at him, he could have wept.

Was she dreaming? Victoria saw her mother, Rebecca, standing over her, beckoning her to get up. She heard her mother say, "Do not fear to live and love."

Victoria's eyes fluttered open, and she didn't know where she was. Fog surrounded her and hid the sun. She could not feel anything above her; underneath and on each side of her was dirt. She lay motionless in the darkness, an unsettling, menacing darkness, full of dancing shadows and the occasional creak and rustle from above her.

Victoria searched desperately for a way to escape what

she could only believe was a hole in the ground.

Suddenly, she remembered what happened; she sat up and at once felt faint and nauseated. Her head hurt, too, and she felt a big lump on the back of her neck near the base.

It must be getting late. Would someone find her?

Would the person who hit her come back to kill her?

The sounds of crunching leaves reached her ears. "Help!" she yelled over and over. The light from a lantern high over the grave dispelled the darkness. A face she didn't recognize appeared above her over the rim of the hole.

"Miss Victoria, my name is Willie. I work at the DuPree stables. You are safe now. More people are nearby. We'll have you out in a minute."

Willie retreated for a second, and Victoria heard him yell, "I found her." More lantern light brightened the area as the search party gathered around the open grave. Allistair appeared out of the fog into the light, and she was glad to see him.

"Victoria, give me your hand," Allistair said with a look of relief on his face as he threw himself on the ground. He helped her climb out. Because of her head wound, she had to quickly sit down so she wouldn't fall.

"Victoria, are you all right? Did you fall in the grave?" Allistair helped her stand up. She swayed and almost fell. He picked her up and carried her out of the graveyard. Allistair put her on his horse, climbed up behind her, and spurred the horse, which charged back to the manor.

Martha had sent for the doctor as soon as the men left

to look for Victoria, so he arrived minutes after she was taken to her rooms. "Victoria, let me introduce you to Dr. Robert Williams," Martha said, as he entered the bedroom.

"Dr. Williams and his wife, Jan, moved to the island six years ago. He established a medical practice to the south of the manor and within walking distance," Martha said. "Dr. Williams is only fifteen years older than Allistair and is up-to-date on the latest patient care."

"Miss Victoria, I'm sorry to meet you at such a time as this. For the next twenty-four hours, if you vomit, Martha will have someone get me. You could have a concussion. You need to rest for a couple of days," said Dr. Williams, after examining her. He left pain medicine and said he'd check on her tomorrow.

"Martha, will you ask Allistair to come to my rooms? I need to tell him what happened in the graveyard," Victoria asked.

Martha returned within a few minutes with Allistair. He was still in his muddy clothes.

"Allistair, I didn't fall in the open grave. Somebody hit me before throwing me in. I was bent over, looking at your father's gravestone, when a man grabbed me from behind. When I awoke, I was lying at the bottom of the hole." Victoria shivered at the memory.

"Bloody hell!" exclaimed Allistair, while his mother sucked in air through clinched teeth.

"I think I know who did it. I have seen the same man three times now. The first time was at my birthday celebration, then that same man was watching me outside the carriage inn on the mainland. Finally, the other day at the lighthouse, I looked down from the gallery, and he was standing near our picnic site. He waved at me before disappearing into the woods," Victoria said.

"Do you think it's Sally's father? Could he have followed me to DuPree Island?" Victoria could not control the fear in her voice. She had told Martha about helping Sally and how the girl's dad threatened to pay her back for stealing his daughter.

Allistair clenched his hands into fists. "I will find out if anyone has seen a stranger on the island. If it is Sally's father, he could be hiding but not for long. Once I tell some of the people to be on the lookout, he'll wish he never set foot on this island. I don't want you going out alone till we find out who is doing these things."

After the mandatory two days of bedrest, Victoria joined the family for dinner.

"Victoria, several of the islanders reported they caught glimpses of a person who appeared to be sneaking around, but a search of the island didn't reveal anyone unknown or suspicious. Of course, the man you saw could have caught the supply ship and is now gone. Please be careful just in case," Allistair said, with a look of worry etched on his face.

Chapter Fourteen: The Importance of Family

A MONTH had gone by since Victoria moved miles away from all she had ever known. She missed her Montgomery family terribly, especially at night because she kept herself busy during the day.

When she felt the need for female companionship, she could talk with Emma and Martha, but sometimes she needed her mother.

In St. Albans, she and her mother had talked every night, when possible, about that day's activities, or made plans for upcoming social and charitable events, or to catch up. Right now, they would be planning for the forthcoming London Season—selecting designs for new dresses and deciding which social entertainments: balls, theater parties, dances, masquerades, and other social pleasures they should and wanted to attend. Mother had written to say, Aunt Yolanda Stanford was taking Victoria's place as the fundraising chairman of the Whitehaven Home board. Victoria was glad someone capable took her place, but she missed being involved.

Lord John joined them for dinner most nights. When he did, Victoria would help him back to his rooms afterward. He protested but obviously looked forward to her tucking him in and fluffing his pillows.

Father asked her to visit him every morning after she finished breakfast. He talked about her mother and made sure she knew as many details about her as possible. When he spoke about Rebecca, he often looked at the wedding portrait on the wall across from his bed. His face always showed a touch of regret. Victoria patted his hand to let him know she understood.

"Your mother had her wedding gown preserved for you to wear when you get married. If you want to wear it, that is," Father said, with a secretive grin on his face. Did he suspect her feelings for Allistair?

"Father, it is a gorgeous wedding dress," she said, looking at the wedding portrait closer. "When I do marry, I will be honored to wear the gown and will think of Mother as I walk down the aisle on your arm." She hoped Allistair asked her to marry him. She knew if or when he did, he would look at her as Father looked at Mother in the portrait.

Since Father missed out on so much during their separation, he asked Victoria to tell him everything about living in London and at the Montgomerys' manor in the country.

Victoria was happy to tell him. As she learned more about the inhabitants of DuPree Island, she knew they were a hardworking group with high regard for her father. Victoria planned to discuss her ideas for helping the families with her father and Allistair soon. For now, she was enjoying her time with her own family.

Victoria's brother, Daniel, was home at last, and she simply adored him. He was a younger version of Father and had many of his mannerisms. Of course, he had cerulean-blue eyes. She and Daniel went riding often and took long walks in the gardens and on the beach.

Victoria could see Daniel's enthusiasm and connection to the island whenever he talked about the people, the wildness of the rocky coastline, and the horses he wanted to train as racing champions.

"I hated that I was sent to boarding school, but soon, I made lots of friends," said Daniel. "School helped me see more of the world than just the island. Father wanted me to continue my education on the mainland, and I now realize why. One day, a long time from now, I will inherit the Barony and will need to take part in the House of Lords. My experiences at boarding school and university will help me make the best decision for the people of England.

"I will have to spend half of the year in London, but the DuPree family has a wonderful townhome in Mayfair. You must stay there when you are in London. We have a full staff and two carriages to take you shopping or to the opera."

"I love attending the opera. The Montgomerys have a townhome in Belgravia. The social activities are such fun." Victoria smiled, remembering the times she accompanied her mother.

"I was surprised when Allistair sent a note, asking me to come home. He has always been there for me as if he were my older brother, and I knew he wouldn't send a message unless necessary. I had finished my exams and planned to take a couple of weeks to explore more of England, Ireland, and Scotland with my best friend, John Wiggington III. Victoria, I know you and John will be fast friends. He is rather amusing and tells terrible jokes. I hope I can invite him to the island so he can meet Father and my long-lost sister," Daniel said, tugging on her hair as only a naughty younger brother would.

"Daniel, do you have a love? Surely someone from university caught your eye." Victoria teased him.

"I could ask you the same, sister. Did you leave someone in London or perhaps the country? You are getting long-in-the-tooth," Daniel laughed, seeing Victoria turn red.

No one had seen the mystery man since the rescue of Victoria from the open grave. Everyone assumed he had left the island. Then a couple of weeks later, a young boy walking through the woods found a makeshift tent. He ran and told his parents about it. Several men went to check it out.

"Victoria, we think we found where the man who attacked you took shelter when he was on the island," Allistair informed her. "He seems to have left in a hurry and hasn't been back. We found papers with instructions telling him to scare you into leaving the island. He would receive money as soon as you went back to St. Albans. There wasn't a signature or any way of telling who hired him."

"Allistair, many people will do anything for money. Do you think Sally's father had the means to hire somebody? He could have stolen the money. I'm afraid the man will come back."

"The whole island is aware of the threat made to you, and we will all keep you safe," he said, giving her a quick hug.

Chapter Fifteen: Martha Confesses

WORK ON THE island took up much of Allistair's time. Victoria usually only saw him at dinner most nights, where he was friendly and considerate to her, but she felt he had changed somehow. Was he fighting his attraction for her?

"I'm going to London to attend a lecture presented by European soil chemists: Sir Humphry Davy from England, Albrecht von Thaer from Prussia, and Justus von Liebig from Germany," said Allistair, one night over pudding.

"Oh? How long will you be away?" asked Father, with a wrinkled brow, cutting his eyes toward Victoria.

"Only for a week," replied Allistair. "I have read many articles and lecture briefs about these chemists and their research. Hopefully, I will learn ways to improve our wheat production. The chemists will show evidence that

118

the exhausted soils of Europe need fresh sources of specific chemicals for crops to flourish again. They say the manure farmers are using isn't enough to produce healthy crops."

Victoria couldn't help wondering if the island gossip about sea gods requiring a child sacrifice in exchange for bountiful crops, and all was true. She mentally shook that thought off. Was it an absurd fable, or did her rescue curse the island?

"Take notes and tell me everything when you return. When I think of the advancements in farming over the last few years, I look forward to using some of them here on the island. Also, the new equipment will save time and keep the workers safe," added Father.

Again, Victoria wondered if her life on the island meant the others were unsafe.

"Just think, soon we will have electric lighting for all the workers' homes, a sewer system, and other inventions here on the island," Allistair said, looking at the electric lighting in the dining room.

Later that night, when leaving Father's rooms, Victoria saw Allistair waiting for her.

"May I escort you to your rooms?" he asked.

"Yes, that would be wonderful," she said, extending her arm to him. "So, you are leaving? A week is a long time to be gone," she said, looking up at his face.

When they reached the door to her rooms, he turned the knob to open it, but instead of walking away, he quickly entered, taking her with him. Allistair shut the door and pulled her close.

"Victoria, I will miss you every minute I am in

London. If you go out of the manor, please ask Daniel to go with you. I don't want to worry about something happening to you while I'm gone. You are too precious to me."

Victoria reached up to touch his face. All she could do was look at him while feeling the heat of his strong body. He put his arms around her, and his lips slowly grazed her forehead, then each cheek, before landing moistly on her lips, which Victoria received willingly.

He released her, then opened the door to see if the hall was empty. "I will leave early in the morning and be back on Friday. Know that every second I am away will be agony. Bye, my love."

Victoria slept with his words in her heart. Over the days, she missed Allistair so much but kept busy visiting with Father, learning more about the workings of the household from Martha, and riding with Daniel every afternoon. As active as she was, she mentally counted the days, hours, and minutes until Allistair would return.

Allistair was motivated about everything he had learned. At dinner, he discussed the lectures with Lord John. They became animated as they talked about wheat production. Victoria ate her dinner, content to listen to these two men she had grown to love in such a brief time.

"Lord John, the researchers' lectures covered things we have already been doing here on the island. We are ahead of other farmers because we add nitrogen, potassium, and lime to our soil. We do need to add phosphoric acid, which should increase our production of wheat even more.

"I talked with one of the researchers while on a lunch break. When I told him that we had some success in increasing our crop yields, he asked me to talk about our processes in one of the next day's sessions. Many attendees took note that we, a local farming enterprise, could show results by already incorporating most of the scientists' suggestions and were having better wheat yields."

Later, when everyone had gone to their rooms, a soft knock signaled someone was at Victoria's door. As she reached for her dressing gown, she saw a note slip underneath. Opening the envelope, she saw the note was from Allistair. He wanted to let her know how much he had missed her. She would keep the note forever.

She was glad Martha had taken over the manor's housekeeping and was now growing closer to Allistair. He told Victoria before Martha became housekeeper, she had almost become a recluse, and they only had dinner together once a week. Now they spent time together often.

While having tea in the drawing room, Victoria mentioned to Martha how much she wished she had known her mother. Something seemed to break in Martha. She spoke in a soft voice with a faraway look in her eyes. Victoria barely heard her, but she was afraid to say anything to interrupt the spell the women seemed to be under.

". . . Paul was working on a piece of broken farming machinery that toppled over and landed on him. Mercifully, he did not suffer. One of his friends, Burt, volunteered to come to our home and tell me the man I loved with all my heart was dead and gone. I will never forget that day. A gentle breeze was blowing flower pods through the air outside my kitchen window. I had forced Allistair to take a nap. He hated doing so, but we were all better when he did. I was peeling potatoes for dinner, humming a love song, and thinking about Paul. Suddenly, the pan in my lap fell to the floor, and potatoes rolled all over the kitchen. I knew that something terrible had happened. Thirty minutes later, Burt was standing at the door.

"Before Burt could say anything, I knew something had happened to Paul. I remember hearing someone screaming. I didn't realize I was making the noise until my cries woke Allistair, and he came running to see what was happening. Burt tried to catch me, but only the cold hard floor did. I fainted; you see. When I awoke, my best friend, Sue, was there beside my bed. She confirmed that Paul was gone."

Martha took a long pause before reaching for Victoria's hand as if needing something to ground her to the earth. Victoria did not speak. She gripped Martha's fingers to let her know she was there for her.

"My world turned gray that day. I knew Allistair needed me, but I could not face him or anyone else. Sue was the only one to whom I could show my despair. Her oldest daughter was fifteen and kept Allistair at their home with all of Sue's children. They were his friends and kept him distracted. Sue told me he cried at night for his mum and usually fell into an exhausted and troubled slumber.

"I couldn't help myself, much less a five-year-old. I was more of a shadow than anyone full of life. I justified my distance in my mind, knowing that Allistair staying with me would only keep the grief close to him. The worst thing was I never got to say goodbye to Paul."

One lone tear slipped down Martha's cheek. When she took a break from her story, Victoria handed her a cup of tea. After taking a couple of sips, Martha continued:

"I owe Lord John for stepping in and taking over the upbringing of Allistair. He needed a father figure, and Lord John filled that void. He hired a tutor, taught him about farming and horses, and how to balance the books. He paid for him to go to university.

"When the manor's housekeeper decided to move back to the mainland to be close to her grandchildren, Lord John saw that I was slowly emerging from my grief. He asked me to fill that position. I have been living here in the manor for five years, which has given me time to work on my relationship with Allistair, too." She finally looked at Victoria with a slight grin. "I didn't mean to burden you with my story, but I feel we are friends now, and I want you to know why I am in my own world sometimes."

"Martha, thank you for telling me. We are friends, and I am glad you live here in the manor. All of this is strange to me. When Allistair arrived in St. Albans on my birthday, my life was turned upside down."

"Speaking of Allistair, I see the way he looks at you. I think you two will be good together."

A heat filled Victoria's face. "We are becoming good friends, I must say. He has made my move to the island easier."

Martha laughed and lifted her teacup to hide her grin. "We'll see how far the friendship goes."

Even after learning more about Martha, Victoria still felt that she was hiding something.

Chapter Sixteen: Secret Engagement

VICTORIA missed Allistair's company for several weeks during the day because he was busy training the new foals. She had to content herself that he was able to join them for dinner most nights. When he finally accompanied them for lunch one day, he told hilarious stories about the young horses.

"They have calm, playful temperaments until you put a leading rope on them. Then they change into bucking demons," Allistair said, crazily moving his hand to demonstrate their bucking movement.

"Rather like the ladies of London—I hear." Joked Daniel.

Everyone at the table laughed as they enjoyed a relaxing lunch.

Allistair touched Victoria's elbow to get her attention.

"Victoria, are you available to go riding with me? I

need to talk to you in private." When she nodded her head, he continued, "I'll go saddle the horses while you change."

"I'll be back in a few minutes," she said, biting her bottom lip with anticipation. When she got to her rooms, she noticed her door was open a couple of inches. She distinctly remembered closing it. She didn't want to keep Allistair waiting, so she pushed it to the back of her mind.

After she changed, she went to tell Father she was going riding with Allistair. She did not want him to worry if he were to ask for her, and no one could find her.

Allistair had both Star and a white stallion ready for their ride. He offered his hand to help her into the saddle.

"You have made me curious about where we are going and what you wish to talk to me about. Is there something wrong with Father?" she said, with worry in her voice.

"No, Victoria, nothing is wrong. I thought we might ride to the waterfall," he said, playfully raising one eyebrow.

Allistair kept his eyes straight ahead, and they did not talk as they left the manor behind. Her mind wandered back to her first visit to the waterfall. Victoria's heart began to beat faster the moment they arrived. Allistair helped her dismount, then taking her hand, he led her to the top of the waterfall. The quietness of the river became louder, cascading to the pool below. For some reason, Victoria got a vision of Esther on the cliff overlooking the sea, about to shove her, to sacrifice her to the sea and the island.

"I don't know how to put this," Allistair said, turning

so swiftly that he almost stumbled over a rock at his feet. "Victoria, I love you. I have ever since I first laid eyes on you in St. Albans. Will you marry me?"

Victoria fought back tears of joy. She knew that she must tell him her feelings, so she moved over closer to him and whispered, "I love you, too."

He kissed her with so much passion; if he had not gripped her tightly, she would've fallen because she became weak in her knees. After she caught her breath, Victoria sat down on a big rock and motioned for him to sit beside her.

"Allistair, please don't misunderstand, but I must ask you not to make plans for now. I am still conflicted. I have just met my father and the rest of the family, and I am not emotionally able to become your wife yet. I want to be your wife and want to have your children, but please be patient with me."

Perhaps she should leave the island, she thought. Perhaps she had brought a curse by her very existence.

"Victoria, my love, I understand how you feel, and I am willing to wait to announce our engagement."

She leaned over and kissed him with warmth and passion. "Thank you," was all she could say before his mouth descended to hers. Eventually, they headed back to the manor, knowing the afternoon would be fading into night soon.

Victoria went to visit her father after changing out of her riding habit. Flushed cheeks and swollen lips from the many kisses Allistair and she shared were evident when she entered his rooms. Father did not mention it, but she could tell he knew something had happened, and Victoria could not hide the joy she felt even in the face of her father's failing health.

"My dear, the fresh air seems to have been good for you," was all he said, before he told her more about their extended family and the many scraps Allistair and Daniel had gotten into when they were younger.

Chapter Seventeen: Black Swan Island

SEVERAL DAYS later, Daniel asked Victoria to honor him with the pleasure of her company on a trip over to Black Swan Island to meet the Wadsworths. He said everyone shortened the name to Swan Island.

Victoria got a shawl and met him on the beach. The trip only took fifteen minutes to row over. Swan Island was rock except for right in the middle. Sir Samuel Wadsworth had commissioned the building of a vast home facing the sizable five-mile-long lake.

Even though Victoria was with Daniel, she couldn't stop thinking about Allistair. He told her about Black Swan Island and the owners during the carriage ride from the Montgomery estate to Southland-on-Sea.

She mentally shook herself to stop thinking of Allistair and listen to Daniel.

". . . Every summer, black swans migrate to the lake; thus the name of the island. Sir Samuel Wadsworth and his daughter, Laura, live on Swan Island in a large manor house," Daniel rambled.

Victoria asked about Laura's mother.

"Five years ago, she committed suicide," said Daniel. "No one knows why because there was not a note or any indication that she felt troubled. I think Laura's mother missed living in London and could not take the isolation. She must've missed her friends and parties that she often attended," he said.

Victoria's heart went out to Laura. She knew that losing one's mother was hard for anyone to endure.

After Daniel secured the boat, they walked across a slight stretch of sand and came upon an almost vertical cliff.

"Sir Samuel hired stonecutters to shape the igneous basalt and granite rock of the cliff into a staircase. The steps are steep with odd twists and turns. I know it isn't noticeable from down here, but the cliff changes directions several times, making it dangerous," Daniel warned her.

Victoria was impressed by the overall design of the property but was concerned about the staircase.

"Is this the only way to the house?" she asked Daniel.

"No, there is another way, but this one is closer to our island. I thought you might enjoy seeing it."

"It's impressive, but I wonder how anyone could climb those steps during a storm or after dark."

"You're right. It's not safe during those conditions,

but you must always be extremely careful. Not having a banister or railing makes climbing to the top tricky. But the descent can be perilous. You can't always judge the depth of each step," Daniel said, before he took her hand to help her up the cliff.

At the top, the sun shone upon a spellbinding body of water surrounded by magnificent trees and ornamental flower beds. As they walked on a gravel pathway, they reached one of three stone bridges built over the lake. They crossed the bridge and walked through a lovely formal garden before reaching the large Georgian country house.

"The house was built of the finest stone masonry. The central five bays consist of three stories with two bay-flanking wings on both sides. At the front, is a central porch with columns. The home stands in a courtyard with the entrance façade facing the lake with an expansive parkland to the rear." Daniel seemed proud to show off his knowledge of Victorian architecture, which Victoria knew he studied at university.

Stone steps led them to massive double doors where a kindly older butler greeted Daniel.

"So good to see you, Phillips. This is Victoria, my sister," said Daniel, beaming.

The butler led them to the drawing room to wait while he announced their arrival to Laura Wadsworth. A few minutes later, Laura came sailing in with a huge basket of flowers.

"Hello. I was in the garden, picking these to brighten the drawing room," Laura said. She put the flowers down on a sideboard then walked over to them.

Daniel bowed to her. "Laura, I know that Allistair told you about my sister and how she has finally come home. So, I thought Victoria might enjoy visiting you. Let me introduce you to one another." Daniel looked flushed, and Victoria attributed that to him helping her up the stone staircase. But was it?

"We came by the stone stairway. I explained how treacherous the steps could be," said Daniel. "Next time I bring her, I will show her the safer side."

Victoria extended her hand, which Laura shook with a firm grip. Fashionably styled chestnut-brown hair, a husky voice, and a ready smile made her enchanting, but her eyes were her best feature. They were a warm brown with specks of gold surrounding the iris. They gave her the appearance of someone who laughed a lot. She didn't seem to be one of the flighty young ladies Victoria had often met at some of the events in London.

"I'm glad you came to visit. What do you think about our rock of an island and especially the stone staircase?" she asked.

"I find the island's deceptiveness rather exciting. Until you climb the stone staircase and come upon the lake and this magnificent home, you think the island is only a big black rock. I can't imagine how long it took to design and carve out such a stunning but dangerous staircase," Victoria said, with a shiver, remembering how scared she felt climbing the stairs even with Daniel there to help her.

"Yes, quite so," said Laura. "A few years ago, Uncle Louie, one of my father's older friends, slipped and fell.

He was lucky that he was almost at the bottom when his foot slipped. Uncle only broke his hip and had some bruises. Our staff usually do not take those stairs and instead use the easier entrance from the sea."

Laura rang for tea, and they enjoyed an hour with her. Before they returned to DuPree Island, Laura's father joined them. Sir Samuel Wadsworth appeared to be nearly fifty with stormy-gray hair and chocolate-brown eyes. He was a friendly man who welcomed Victoria to his home and showed her the elaborately designed gardens.

As they walked back to the beach, Daniel seemed excited to find out her opinion of the Wadsworths. "Isn't having such nice neighbors exciting?"

"They are a lovely family, and I'm sure Laura and I will become close. Unless that position belongs to you, little brother," she said, resting her hand on his arm.

Daniel stiffened and tried to cover up his embarrassment by changing the subject. "Once a year, both families hold a magnificent ball and invite family and friends from the mainland to attend. Most of whom spend two weeks with us. We take turns hosting. This year is the Wadsworths' turn. Both houses have many activities planned for entertainment and will be packed with guests. I can't wait to introduce you to our extended family and my university friends. Doesn't that sound thrilling?"

"I look forward to the ball and, of course meeting your friends. I want to know all the stories that only they can tell me about you." She laughed while he looked nervous.

When they reached the stone staircase, Victoria was

glad Daniel cautiously helped her descend them. Halfway down, she felt her foot slip. She screamed as her shoe came off and plummeted down the cliff until no longer visible. Daniel snatched her from the edge.

"I can truthfully say I never want to take this staircase by myself. Thank you for saving me, brother of mine."

When they reached the beach at the bottom, Daniel ran and retrieved her shoe. "It's worse for wear, I fear," he said, "but should make walking on the rocky beach easier."

She hugged him before stepping into the boat for their return trip.

Chapter Eighteen: Who is in the Garden?

THE MISSING piece that Victoria always felt while growing up as an only child in London was filled by her father and brother. She missed her Montgomery family so much at times, but her DuPree family helped her realize how lucky she was to have two families who loved her. She enjoyed exploring the island with Allistair, and their love grew daily.

Late one night, Victoria woke up hot; opening a window, she moved a chair where she could look out at the formal gardens and enjoy the night breeze. She heard the soft cough of somebody down below. She saw the silhouette of an older, stooped-shouldered woman slowly walking through the gardens. The woman stopped below the window and lifted her chin as if seeing Victoria hiding in the dark room. Who was this woman? Could she see her in the window?

Victoria had met everyone living in the manor except for her grandmother. If Esther was locked in the tower with a companion to watch her, could she have gotten out? Victoria would inquire about the matter the next time she saw Allistair.

Because everyone was helping with the wheat harvest, Victoria forgot to ask Allistair who could be walking in the gardens at night. Most of the men were out in the fields for up to ten hours daily. She was glad the women had asked her to help deliver lunch to the workers. They set up tables in a central place, and the men stopped at twelve sharp to eat. When Victoria saw their camaraderie and jovial antics, she grinned so much her face ached. Harvesting took a week to finish.

A few nights later, Victoria awoke from an unsettling dream about the mysterious woman she had seen walking in the gardens below. She felt drawn to look out her window at the giant harvest moon. A snapping of a twig drew her attention to the right corner of the gardens, where a large stone bench sat. She saw the same woman walking in the gardens again. When the woman turned toward the manor, the moonlight clearly revealed the person's face. Victoria saw her grandmother, Esther, for the first time since returning to the island.

Esther kept glancing toward her window. She did not resemble a deranged or evil person as Victoria had imagined her looking by now. Victoria felt the need to go to Esther. Not taking time to think, she grabbed her robe and put on walking boots.

Victoria tiptoed downstairs as quietly as possible and exited the manor, using the door closest to the gardens. Victoria stepped onto the gravel walkway leading toward the stone bench. Esther stopped and turned her way.

"Grandmother," Victoria whispered.

"At long last. I have wanted to see you but wasn't allowed." Esther crept toward her.

"I thought you were confined to the tower rooms. Seeing you from my window, I had to come down here to meet you."

"They now allow me to walk in the gardens to get fresh air and exercise a couple of nights a week.

"Hearing you had returned to the island pleased my heart. I do not remember anything after picking you up to go outside until your father grabbed you from my arms. I cannot even recall walking to the edge of the sea. Everything before and after remains clear in my head. I am so sorry that you did not grow up on the island because of me, and most of all, you did not get to know your mother. Can you forgive me for what I tried to do years ago?" Esther cried.

Victoria did not know how to respond. Should she risk hugging her?

"It is, um, good to finally meet you." Victoria eased a few steps closer. Esther sat down on the bench a few feet

137

away and asked about Victoria's life in London. That was a good place to start, Victoria imagined, as she told her of her Montgomery parents and some of the things she did in the country as well. Her pulse still pounded with uncertainty.

"Oh, that is so good to hear, Victoria," Esther said, as if seeing with her old eyes a life she had missed behind the walls of a locked tower. Her gnarled fingers clenched and released the rim of the stone bench.

"If you want, dear, you can meet me here in the gardens on any of the nights you are available. I have so missed talking to someone besides Susie and Martha," Esther said, with a look of hope.

Victoria did not commit to meeting her, but something compelled her to start a routine of sneaking out when she knew Esther was in the gardens. She wanted, or more accurately, she needed to meet her there so they could get closer. From her volunteer work in London, Victoria remembered the doctors explaining that some people can completely block any episodes of mental imbalance. The person could shut down and go into a comatose state if they remembered something they did to harm others.

Victoria did not tell anyone that she was secretly meeting Esther. If asked to stop, she would have to disagree. Most Tuesdays and Thursdays, Victoria visited with her grandmother in the gardens. They either sat on the stone bench or in the gazebo and talked for an hour at least.

One night, Esther spoke about her husband. ". . .

Being separated from William for such a long time was so difficult. I wasn't even present when he died." A solitary tear traveled down her wrinkled cheek.

Victoria reached for Esther's cold hand, which felt natural, but she quickly released it. At least they were bonding.

"Life was dreamlike when I first married and moved to DuPree Island," continued Esther, with a mellow crackle in her voice. "John was my greatest joy. He was the only child that lived out of six pregnancies. He even said he wanted to marry me when he grew up. I spent more time with him than his father. The island was a wilderness when Lord William received it from Queen Victoria. He had to work all day and into the night to build the manor, clear fields and woods for the farming land, and construct the horse stables.

"I was pleased when John found a great woman for his wife. Rebecca was a good daughter-in-law and treated me with much respect. Things changed when Rebecca told everyone she was having a baby. The fear of losing the little bundle of joy hit me hard. I didn't want to become attached to a baby that might die. I didn't!" She doubled over as if in agony.

"Grandmother, I'm sorry that you lost five babies, and I understand having the fear that I would die as well. I don't comprehend why you tried to throw me in the sea, however." Victoria had to be honest with her, and she hoped Esther would be frank with her as well.

"I only remember when John snatched you from my arms, stopping me before I could sling you into the sea far below. It took a long time to get out of the fog surrounding me before I could think straight. Victoria, I do not know why I snapped."

Chapter Nineteen: Misplaced Items

THE FOLLOWING week, strange things started to happen. Father had given Victoria her mother's jewelry. Most of the pieces were locked in the family safe, but a few were kept in her rooms. She got ready for dinner and went to her jewelry box to pick out pieces to enhance her dress.

"One of my favorite rings is missing!" Victoria gasped. "Where is the one Father said my mother always wore? I know I left the ring in the middle of the top tray." Victoria usually wore the ring unless going riding around the island. She searched her rooms and then retraced her steps to the last place she remembered wearing the ring, but she couldn't find it anywhere.

Victoria asked everyone if they had seen the ring, but no one had. The next morning, when she opened the jewelry box, she saw the ring. Other pieces taken, moved, or missing would eventually reappear in different areas throughout the manor. The same thing happened to fans, wraps, and even a pair of shoes she owned.

Each night she wrote to the Montgomerys about that day's occurrences. She wanted them to know she was well and was enjoying everything on the island. She marked each page with the date. It helped her, and hopefully, them get a good glimpse of each day. Every other Friday morning, she would seal the letter and leave it on the silver tray in the foyer. The butler put all the mail in the mailbag and had it taken to the supply ship for delivery to the mainland.

Several times, Victoria noticed the letters in her rooms were not in date order. She kept all her letters in the wardrobe in her riding-hat box. She was the only one who knew where she kept them, so she must have gotten them out of order.

Victoria soon felt no one believed her when she asked about her missing personal items. Not wanting anyone to think she was losing her mind or wonder if she had inherited her grandmother's mental imbalance, she quit mentioning anything about missing items.

Chapter Twenty: Broken Buggy Axle

AFTER MEETING most of the islanders and seeing ways to improve their lives, Victoria decided now was the time to talk to her father. After dinner, when she and Allistair escorted him to his rooms, she asked to discuss ideas she wanted to execute on the island.

"I have noticed several families that have needs that I want to remedy. I want to deliver baskets of food or send a handyman to repair the homes of those who cannot make the repairs themselves. Do you approve, Father?" Victoria asked, hoping he would think it was a great idea.

"Victoria, I am glad this is something you feel you want to do. Your mother was always helping people. She knew when each person's birthday was and had our cook pack a basket with special foods, including a birthday cake. She knew who was sick and would visit and take a care basket, including her special soup recipe. She had our carpenter fix anything that the homeowner could not do themselves. I am glad to give my blessing for you to take on this endeavor."

"Thank you, Father. Martha also told me about my mother doing these things. I want to continue her legacy."

"I agree with your father; this will show the people of the island that we care about them," Allistair said.

"I'll need a buggy to make the deliveries. Is Mother's still available?" she asked, already thinking of ways to accomplish everything she wanted to do.

"Yes. If I remember correctly, the buggy is in the big barn next to the stables. Look at it and see if it needs any repairs before you make your first trip. You can use one of the ponies, too. Ask the stable manager for a gentle one since the road to the workers' homes can be bumpy." Father seemed pleased she was taking on this project.

Over the next week, Victoria put her plan into action. As soon as her mission started, she knew that the word would spread. Victoria knew about checking a buggy to make sure everything was in working order. She had used a similar buggy for deliveries on the Montgomery estate. The seat was wide enough for two. Since Emma was an island native, Victoria asked her to accompany her on the first delivery. She shared Victoria's excitement for helping those in need.

The day before they planned to make their first deliveries, Emma met her in the hall. She had a nice-looking gentleman with her. "Victoria, I want to introduce my brother, Henry, to you. He just returned from serving in Her Majesty's Naval Service in the West Indies."

"How do you do, Henry? I'm sure Emma told you about me and my homecoming after many years in London," she said, extending her hand to him.

"Pleased to meet you, Victoria. I was twelve years old when you were born and remember your mother. She was so cordial to everyone. My condolences." His smile didn't seem to reach his eyes. Victoria blamed that on the deep sunburn that created creases around his temples. She had heard the harsh sun in the West Indies, and the wind on board a ship could chap the skin.

"I'm sure your father is glad you are home," Victoria said.

"My mother died years ago. I was only twelve at the time. Emma's mother was the second Mrs. Jonas. She was so nice to me when she married my father. We still grieve her passing," Henry said, putting an arm around Emma's shoulders.

The next day, Emma and Victoria headed out with a loaded buggy. Their pony was such a gentle soul and seemed to enjoy slowly taking the trail toward the workers' homes. At one point, they had to travel close to the cliff's edge overlooking the sea. The smell of the salty air was invigorating, and the pony picked up speed.

They were almost past the closest edge to the sea when Victoria heard the splitting of wood. The buggy tilted on the side nearest the drop-off. They screamed, which startled the pony who tried to run, but the wheel nearest the seat broke off. Seated farthest from the sea, Victoria gripped the pony reins to keep him from bolting, which might have caused the buggy to tip, and Emma could have fallen over the cliffside.

Quickly, Victoria helped Emma out of the buggy just as the broken wheel rolled over the edge. Over the cries of the seagulls, the wood crashed with a thud on the rocks below.

Emma clung to Victoria and cried. She was shaking so much Victoria led her a safe distance away and made her sit down.

"The wheel was in good order yesterday. Why did it break completely off?" Victoria asked. "I checked the buggy, and everything seemed in good repair." Shaking as well, she sat beside Emma until she felt she could walk back to the manor to get help.

Emma would not stay behind, so they started walking back together. They were halfway there when Henry came riding toward them. He knew they were going to make deliveries. They had talked about it when Emma introduced them the day before.

"Ladies, why are you walking?" Henry jumped down and at once took his sister's hands.

Emma explained about the wheel breaking off and falling to the rocks below.

"You are shaking. Let me get help from the manor. Sit here under this tree, and I will be back as fast as possible," said Henry.

Soon they heard both horses and another buggy headed their way. Allistair and Henry were riding in front and reached them first. They dismounted and came to check on the two ladies. Allistair stopped in front of Victoria and offered his hand to lift her from the ground. "Have you been injured?" He looked from her to Emma as if he needed to make sure they were okay. Victoria thought she saw the leathery wrinkles deepen on Henry's face. Did he see that Allistair loved her? They were trying to keep that a secret for a while longer.

Allistair took her sidesaddle up on his horse while Henry did the same with his sister. They refused to let them continue their mission of visiting the families.

"You have had a serious scare and need to rest," said Allistair. "The trauma will set in later today, so let us take you home."

He pulled Victoria close as they galloped to the manor. She was glad he thought of the manor as their home. Victoria leaned back against Allistair's chest and knew that she was safe with him.

"My love, I'm so glad you were not harmed. I will have someone check out the buggy and see why the wheel broke. You told us last night at dinner that you inspected the buggy and saw nothing wrong. I'm surprised an accident at that drop-off hadn't happened before. I will personally see that the buggy is safe for use. Also, I will have workers create a path for buggies at least ten feet from the cliff drop-off. As noble as this mission is, I hope you will reconsider undertaking such a task." Allistair whispered in her ear as they rode.

Victoria wanted to protest but felt perhaps she had misread his implications and was still shaken from the fact that Emma almost died before the mission began.

"Two workers will unload the small buggy and deliver the food baskets. You labeled each one, making their task easier for delivering to the right people. The other two men will patch the buggy before leading the pony back to the stables." Allistair tightened his hold on her waist.

When they reached the manor, Emma and Victoria went to their rooms to lie down. Since they were mentally as well as physically spent, they decided to have dinner in their rooms. Victoria barely recalled Allistair opening the door and tiptoeing to the bed to softly kiss her lips.

Chapter Twenty-One: Sinking Rowboat

THE FOLLOWING morning, Allistair pulled Victoria aside at the bottom of the staircase.

"Dearest, I cannot be sure, but somebody seemed to have intentionally cut the axle holding the wheel enough so it would eventually break. Are you sure you checked out the buggy thoroughly? Do you know there is an axle connected to the wheels and makes them turn? I will show you where the axle is located after it is fixed.

"Also, we need to rethink how your mission to help those in need is carried out. After you have a list of who will get baskets, meet with the cook to discuss what you want in each. Here is the change I highly suggest: Let several stable hands load the buggy and make the deliveries for you. You will still get the credit for delivering the baskets, but those workers will know how to manage any problems that might occur."

Victoria refused to answer and walked away. She was sure he was surprised by her action. Still shaken from yesterday, she was angry that Allistair thought she did not know about axles. How dare any man think himself more intelligent in these matters.

"*Argh*! I need to change my clothes and take a rowboat out to work off my anger," she muttered. "Rowing always helps when I'm upset. The island men don't think a lady can do that either. Because I don't wear trousers doesn't mean I'm helpless. I guess they think I tried to kill Emma. They'll want to lock me up in the tower, too."

As she headed to her rooms to change, she looked forward to being on the water. Opening the door, Victoria caught a glimpse of Henry and Emma coming down the hall and thought she heard Emma calling out to her. She quickly shut herself in her rooms to avoid anyone else seeing her in a foul mood.

After changing, Victoria left the manor and dared anyone to stop or question her. In her desire to see the other side of the island from the water, she selected the first small rowboat nearest the boardwalk. Victoria was rusty in her rowing skills at first. But the island was so beautiful from the water, she was already relaxing. The seagulls were enjoying the high drafts, and their cries competed with the crashing of the waves.

Wanting a better view of the manor house perched upon the most prominent hill, Victoria rowed farther out to sea before turning right to start her journey to circle the island. Water lapped against her boots before she noticed the boat was beginning to sink. Victoria yelled for help but knew the chances that someone would hear her cries were slim. She noticed bubbles rising from one specific spot in the boat and saw a hole allowing water to seep in. Victoria tore strips from her petticoats and shoved the fabric to plug the hole, breaking several fingernails as water continued to rise in the boat.

She sucked the blood from her fingers. She didn't want to attract sharks. Her chances in the freezing water with her heavy clothing were not good at all.

Chapter Twenty-Two: Not Accidents

INALLY, someone on the island noticed her frantically waving. Victoria was glad because the wind was overpowering her screams from reaching the shore. *Was it the sea gods finally taking her into her watery grave?* Someone ran down the boardwalk, jumped in a rowboat, and headed toward her location. She saw Allistair running as fast as possible before jumping from the cliff into the water. He reached her first as the boat sank. With his help, she swam to the rescue rowboat, which soon got them to the beach. If she had been on the other side of the island, she would not have had a chance of surviving because of the vertical cliffs, and the likelihood that someone would be there was improbable.

Victoria was shivering, but soon others ran down the hillside with blankets while Allistair pulled her into his embrace.

"I am not causing this, and I am fully capable of doing things for myself." Victoria pulled away and looked him in the eyes.

"So, you *are* angry with me? I knew something was wrong when you walked away this morning as I cautioned you about the buggy axle. On my way to find you to talk, something on the water alerted me—my love waving for help; my heart almost stopped. Sweetness, my fear was great that I wouldn't reach you in time." Allistair whispered with a shaky voice. "I never intended to paint you as incapable. My concern for you became a little overbearing; forgive me. We will discuss everything after you get out of these wet clothes."

"Allistair, you need to know that before you saved me, I noticed a round hole in the bottom of the boat that was not visible when I first got in. Rowing out farther than I would normally have to see more of the island, I noticed water rising through that hole. I tore my petticoats, hoping I could plug it, but the water kept rising," she whispered.

With a frown, Allistair motioned for a man to come closer.

"Johnny, when the beach is empty of most people, please take Tom and Joe and recover the sunken rowboat. When you have it, send word to me. I want to see why the boat sank," he said quietly. "Act normal, and don't let anyone else look at the boat but me."

Allistair helped get Victoria to the manor and handed her over to his mother. Martha sprang into action and ordered a hot bath.

"Victoria, let's get you in the tub and then some dry clothes because a few minutes in the chilly water can lead to pneumonia." Martha gently led her up the stairs. "I will have soup and hot tea delivered to your rooms. You will be warm and cozy soon."

When she reached the second-floor landing, Victoria looked down into the foyer and saw Allistair throw her a kiss before quickly leaving through a side door. That warmed her more than hot water and clothes could ever do.

When she was snug in her bed, Emma rushed in. "Victoria, I just heard about you almost drowning. I ran back to the manor as fast as I could to check on you. I was visiting my father who has a head cold. Henry had just told me about our father when we saw you earlier. You were mumbling to yourself. I called after you, but you didn't respond. We were both going to check on dad, but Henry remembered something he needed to do at the stables. He's hoping to get back his job of training horses."

"Emma, I must have hit a submerged rock that I didn't see. I was able to catch someone's attention. Allistair jumped in and saved me. Martha got me into a hot bath and is going to bring me soup in a few minutes."

Later that afternoon, sitting in front of the roaring fire in her bedroom, a soft knock sounded on Victoria's door. Allistair had come to check on her.

"My darling, I have been so worried. I'm sorry I had to leave, but I knew my mother would take great care of you. Are you feeling well? Do you have a fever?" Allistair asked, raising her hand to his lips.

"I don't have any ill effects from my experience in the sea," she said, sitting up taller.

"I wanted to stay with you," said Allistair, "but I needed to find out why the rowboat sank. Johnny always makes sure all the boats are in good working order. He checked the rowboats yesterday afternoon, and all were seaworthy. The boat you took out was nearest the boardwalk and would naturally be the first anyone would choose," he said, as his blue eyes dulled. "After raising the boat from the sea bottom, I met Johnny on the beach, and we both saw the perfectly round hole you mentioned. There were remnants of something lodged in the opening. Some scoundrel drilled through the bottom then used some substance as a filler, which matched the same color as the aged wood of the boat." Allistair's lips formed a grimace.

"I told you somebody is doing these things to me. I'm not crazy or incapable," said Victoria.

"I'm so sorry I didn't take your missing items seriously either. I do not doubt your abilities and do not want to scare you, but we need to be vigilant in keeping you safe. Let someone know if you leave the manor. I have decided to secretly move into the bedroom directly beside yours. If you call out, I can be here quickly if you need me."

Allistair joined her on the settee and held her hand.

"I can only stay with you a few more minutes before someone comes to check on you. I have not told your father about you or the boat. I think you should take a nap before dinner, then we both should tell him. Lord John will be upset if he finds out from someone else. Let's tell him and everyone else you hit a submerged rock. Until we know more, you and I should be the only ones who know about the hole. I can trust Johnny to keep quiet.

"The axle and boat incidents were not accidents, but we don't want whoever sabotaged them to know that we are aware. Somebody is trying to scare you away." Allistair looked worried.

Chapter Twenty-Three: Secret Places

SOMETHING woke Victoria. She heard the faint clicking of metal against metal. Where was it coming from?

Because the drapes were open, the moonlight helped her eyes adjust to the room's darkness, and she saw the shape of somebody tiptoeing around her vanity. The sound she heard was the click of jewelry hitting jewelry. Knowing Allistair was next door, she let out a blood-curdling scream. The shadow froze for a second then turned toward her as if to attack her. But instead, he touched the wall next to the fireplace causing a hidden panel to open. The shadow went through the opening and disappeared as the panel closed.

After that panel shut, another one on the opposite side of her sitting area opened to admit Allistair. He carried a lit candle. He first looked toward her bed to make sure she was okay. When he saw her sitting up, he then searched the room for an intruder.

"Victoria, what is wrong? I was reading when I heard you scream," he said, advancing to her bedside.

"Allistair, somebody was in my room going through my jewelry box. The noise awoke me. I could only see a shadow. When I screamed, he opened a panel near the fireplace and disappeared. Wait, did you come through a panel over there, too?" she asked, perplexed.

"Victoria, when the manor was built, several panels were included for a quick escape if ever needed."

"Why didn't you tell me about the panels? Seeing the second one open, I thought the 'shadow person' was coming back through a different opening."

"Victoria, I'm sorry I didn't tell you. I knew about the panel I came through. It opens to your room only. That's why I moved into that room so I could get to you quickly. I did not know about the one near the fireplace. I am going to see where that panel leads. I'll be back in a couple of minutes," Allistair said, moving toward the fireplace.

"Please be safe," she said, as she heard someone outside her door.

"Victoria, I heard a scream. It's Martha. Are you all right? Can I come in?"

"Just a minute, and I'll unlock the door." She turned on a bedside lamp, put on her dressing gown, and reached the door as Allistair disappeared behind the panel near the fireplace.

"Martha, I'm sorry, I had an unpleasant dream. I think I was overwrought by the events yesterday. I didn't mean to disturb you. Please go back to bed. I'll see you in the morning."

As Martha turned to go back to her room, Victoria heard the faint sound of the panel opening. For a second, she thought it was the "shadow" coming back. Seeing Allistair, she quickly closed the bedroom door and turned the lock.

Allistair reached for her and held her tight. "There's a passageway behind that panel, but I found nothing nor no one. I'll conduct a thorough search in the morning. In the meantime, help me move a heavy piece of furniture in front of the panel near the fireplace."

Together they moved the wardrobe to that side of the room. Victoria felt much safer. Allistair kissed her and said he would see her in the morning before heading back to the panel on the wall of her sitting area.

"Allistair, don't leave me tonight." She fought a rising panic. "I need you."

"I will stay here on the settee then. Let me get a pillow and blanket." He returned in mere seconds.

By then, Victoria had removed her dressing gown and was in bed. Patting the mattress, she said, "Allistair, please hold me. No one will know you stayed." She moved over to make room for him and even pulled back the covers.

Allistair eased over to her. "Sweetness, if I lie with you, it will drive me mad with desire. Has anyone told you about lovemaking between a man and a woman? Do you know how babies are made?"

"I'm not a child; I know a lot from my work with unwed mothers and living on a country estate. I know a man and woman lie together after marriage. Also, I know many lower-class women get pregnant without having a husband. Seeing animals mate on the country estate was strange to me until I asked a stable hand about it, and he told me what was happening," Victoria explained to Allistair, with a touch of shyness and a shiver of anticipation.

"Victoria, I love you and am so pleased to have you as my bride-to-be, but I don't want to do anything before our wedding that you think isn't right for us to do."

When she once again motioned him closer, he removed his dressing gown and sat down upon the bed. Lifting the covers, he pulled his legs up to slide them under the bedspread.

Victoria had never seen a man's legs uncovered. His were muscular from working with horses and on the farm. The soft covering of dark hairs seemed to be calling out for her to touch them. She resisted that impulse, but as her eyes slowly moved up his body, she could not keep from reaching out to touch his bare chest. Her fingers gently stroked the splattering of hair they found there. The texture was coarse but soft at the same time. She so wanted to follow the hair traveling down his torso and hiding beneath his underpants.

As her hand moved lower, Allistair reached out to stop her. He released a low moan and, through gritted teeth, said, "Darling, if your hand moves any lower, I will not be able to stop. I know we both want to consummate our love on our wedding day, but if you want, I can give you a sample of what to expect."

"Yes, please. I need you, but I am not sure what that means. I'm yours for whatever you want to teach me."

Allistair moved over and kissed her with such passion she felt she would burst. He asked if she were ready, and when she nodded, he leaned down and took one of her breasts in his mouth. How one had escaped her nightgown, she did not know, but both breasts were in full view. The sensations were too much to endure. There seemed to be a direct line from her breasts to the secret place between her legs. As he licked and sucked one breast while kneading the other one, she started to throb below. She could feel wetness gathering there also.

Slowly Allistair raised her gown and ran his hand down her stomach, which quivered, sending more sensations to the junction between her legs. As his fingers skimmed the hair covering her secret place, she rocked and moaned more and more. When he eased his finger between the folds, she felt as if she were about to soar to the stars. Victoria reached out to stop him, but instead, she helped him move his hand closer.

"Please, I'm about to faint from the sensations. Is this normal? Should this be happening to me?" She cried out breathlessly.

"Victoria, this is only a foretaste of the pleasures of our coupling on our wedding night. Hold onto me, and feel the love," he said as he rubbed a spot she did not know she had. The friction increased as she bucked and thrashed with each pulse.

Victoria thought she would die, but as she felt she could not take the sensations anymore, she reached the stars. Allistair seemed to anticipate her reaction and kissed her to keep anyone in the manor from hearing her scream. He pulled her close until she stopped quivering.

"Did you feel the same sensations?" she panted, touching his face.

"That will happen on our wedding night. You will also enjoy more wonderful sensations then. This was the start of how we will consummate our love and eventually bring children into the world."

"Thank you for such wonderful feelings," Victoria mumbled, as she slipped into a peaceful sleep with her head on Allistair's chest, listing to his heartbeats.

Chapter Twenty-Four: Falling Angels

A KNOCK on her door alarmed Victoria. She turned to look for Allistair and found that his side of the bed was empty. Allistair made sure to leave no sign that he had stayed with her last night.

She quickly pulled on her dressing gown and unlocked the door.

"I am here to help you dress. You have never locked your door before," said Emma.

"I must have turned the lock because I was so drained. I still cannot believe I hit a hidden rock while in a rowboat. You know I am incredibly good at rowing, but I do not know the waters here. I am glad I was rescued before my heavy skirts could pull me under."

"Victoria, I am so upset, knowing how close you came to—you are my best friend, and I cannot lose you. Never go out without someone accompanying you, please." Emma gently smoothed out a new day dress on the bed with extra care.

Victoria felt her face grow hot when she saw Allistair at the breakfast table. While everyone else was making selections from the buffet, he gave her a sly wink before pouring two cups of coffee. One he offered to her.

"Good morning, my dear. Oh my, you must still have a fever; your cheeks are so red. Let me check." Martha reached out and placed the back of her hand on Victoria's forehead.

Allistair lowered his head to conceal the grin on his face. Daniel was excited about a new foal that was born a couple of days ago. He felt the horse could grow up to be the next winner of the Grand National. He and Allistair debated the foal's name when Victoria spoke up and suggested "Daniel's Choice," which caused everyone to laugh. But the name seemed to grow on them, and finally, it became the foal's official name. Victoria was glad to be a part of this family and looked forward to many more such gatherings.

Allistair checked out the hidden passageway, which ended with another panel opening near the servants' staircase. Having the wardrobe block the hidden panel in her room gave Victoria peace of mind. Allistair being next door helped her rest except when she thought about her pre-wedding introduction to lovemaking a few nights ago. Then she had trouble sleeping from wanting him with her. Allistair kept the panel between their rooms open but would not stay in her rooms.

"Sweetheart, I don't know if I can resist making love to you if I join you in your bed again. I want us to wait until our wedding. I promise we will both have a memorable time," Allistair said.

Victoria had not told anyone about meeting her grandmother. The first Tuesday, after somebody was in her room, Victoria did not feel comfortable leaving the manor late at night. She did not have a way to let her grandmother know, but they had already discussed the possibility that one of them might not be able to come every time.

Victoria awoke with a start. She thought she heard something fall hard to the ground outside her window. Getting out of bed, she looked out the glass pane and saw Esther with Daniel. They were staring at the ground to see what had fallen when suddenly they looked up as a giant stone statue tumbled past Victoria's window. Everything happened so quickly; she thought she must be dreaming.

Victoria saw Daniel push Esther out of the way, but he couldn't move fast enough before the falling stone knocked him to the ground. Victoria screamed, which brought Allistair running into her room. All she could do was clasp her hand over her mouth to stop the shrieks and point out the window.

Chapter Twenty-Five: Next Steps

ALLISTAIR looked out and saw Daniel lying on the ground. He quickly unlocked the bedroom door, and Victoria could hear him running down the stairs. He yelled for the butler and Martha. Victoria grabbed her dressing gown but forgot her shoes in her hurry to get to Daniel. At the top of the stairs was Father's manservant heading her way. She asked him to check on Father, but he let her know Lord John was still sound asleep. She knew some of his medicines kept him sedated at night. Thank goodness.

When Victoria reached the gardens, she saw that Grandmother's companion was holding her back from getting in the way as Allistair checked on Daniel. Emma's brother, Henry, appeared from around the corner of the house.

"Henry, please go get the doctor," Allistair said.

Victoria was so glad their island was large enough for a doctor to live close by.

"There don't seem to be any broken bones other than one of his arms," said Allistair.

Esther was as white as a sheet. He asked her companion to take her to her rooms in the tower.

"Esther, we will make sure you know how Daniel is as soon as the doctor checks him out. Now please go with Sally and try not to worry.

"Victoria, Daniel is a strong young man, but I do not want to move him until the doctor examines him. Please go in with Emma. You need shoes. You could catch a cold."

Victoria looked down and, for the first time, felt the cold, wet ground under her feet. She let Emma lead her back inside.

After she changed into warmer clothes and a pair of shoes, the chill from walking outside without shoes abated. Victoria knew she was trembling, not just from the cold. How seriously hurt was Daniel?

Waiting for the doctor to examine and treat Daniel seemed to take a long time. Allistair stayed with Daniel to be of any assistance to Dr. Williams.

"Miss Victoria, do not worry; your brother will rest until later this morning. A sedative will help with the pain. He has a fractured arm which has been set. So far, no internal injuries are evident. If Daniel doesn't get a fever, he should make a full recovery," Dr. Williams said to Victoria. "I will come back after daybreak to check on him."

Victoria needed to see Daniel for her own peace of mind. She quietly opened the door to his private quarters and touched his forehead to see if he felt hot. Thank goodness he did not. Daniel opened his eyes a little, then closed them again. He mumbled, "Laura?" Victoria would have to ask him about his feelings for their neighbor when he was no longer on bed rest.

As she sat by his bed, she had just nodded off when Allistair softly kissed her, causing her to jerk awake.

"Sorry I gave you a fright, sweetness, but you looked so pretty sitting there. Come out into the hallway so we can talk without disturbing Daniel." Allistair helped her to stand.

"Victoria, what caused you to look out your window?"

"I heard something fall and hit the ground below. I looked out the window and heard Esther and Daniel talking in the gardens. A large stone statue fell past my window from above. I at once looked down and saw Daniel push Esther out of the way, but he wasn't able to move fast enough to keep himself from harm."

"It's too dark tonight, but tomorrow I will see if any other statues are loose and make sure they are made secure. My love, why don't you go to bed, and I will sit with Daniel? If anything changes, I will wake you. Make sure you lock your door." He kissed her before walking her to her rooms.

The sun was high in the sky when Emma entered Victoria's rooms. "Allistair said to leave you alone. But I thought you would want to know: Daniel woke up a few minutes ago, and the doctor has already been here. He left instructions with Martha for Daniel's care. He said to make sure he takes it easy for a couple of days before trying to do anything."

Victoria dressed before first going to see Father. She was worried that he would be upset by the night's events and that he could not help. "Father, I would have been here to see you earlier, but Allistair asked Emma to let me sleep. Has he told you about Daniel?"

"Allistair came early and told me everything about last night. I am glad Daniel is okay. I will visit him after lunch," Father said, with a frown between his eyebrows.

They talked for a few minutes, then his manservant arrived with his lunch tray. The scent of roast chicken made her remember she had not had breakfast. She left Father and went in search of lunch.

Martha ushered her to a chair and put a plate of delicious-looking food in front of her. Victoria ate while going over last night's events in her mind. Suddenly, she remembered she had not said a word since entering the dining room.

"I'm sorry, Martha. The food was so good. Have you heard the reason one of the roof statues fell?"

"Allistair is checking out the roof right now. We'll just have to wait. He shouldn't be gone too long," Martha said, offering her another roll.

"I wish I had been awake when the doctor visited," Victoria said, eating the second roll without even realizing it.

"I was with the doctor when he checked on Daniel.

He asked him questions to evaluate his memory, had him move his arm and legs to see his range of motion, and performed other tests to rule out any injuries other than his right arm," Martha chuckled.

"What's funny?" Victoria asked.

"After the checkup, Daniel said, 'God sent the angels to get me, but the one that hit me misunderstood and was *out to get me* instead.' He laughed with us until he moved his arm the wrong way. Victoria, he's going to be fine."

She was glad Daniel had a sense of humor about the situation, but she could not help wondering whether the falling stone was an accident.

After lunch, Victoria went to Daniel's room and found Allistair sitting beside the bed. He quickly rose to let her sit and put his hand on her shoulder.

"Daniel, I just found out I have a brother, and I thought I lost you last night."

"Do not worry about me. The angel is the only one who can't be fixed." Daniel tried again to make light of the situation.

Allistair reached over and wiped the final tear rolling down her cheek. She looked at him with a questioning glance.

"Victoria, I told Daniel about our secret last night after the doctor set his arm, and his pain was so great. I know you wanted to wait, but I thought getting his mind on something instead of his arm would help him." Allistair caressed her cheek.

"I am so excited for you two. I can't wait for you to give me nieces and nephews to play with and spoil,"

Daniel said.

She could see the natural color returning to his face, and his jovial attitude set her mind at ease.

"Daniel, please keep this a secret. I want to tell Father myself when the time is right. Speaking of Father, has he visited you? He was so worried."

They talked for a bit longer, then Allistair walked with her to her rooms.

"I have news for you about the statue that fell. Go inside, and I will come through the panel in a few minutes," Allistair said, walking away.

Within five minutes, the panel opened to reveal Allistair. "Victoria, let's sit here on the settee. I went on the roof this morning and found all the other statues in perfect condition. None were loose in any way. The one that fell had obvious signs of being tampered with and was deliberately pushed from the roof."

She was shocked and could only stare at Allistair.

"Victoria, I think somebody was trying to kill either Daniel or Esther. Do you know why they were out in the gardens late at night?"

"Allistair, I meant to tell you that I have been meeting my grandmother twice a week in the gardens. I saw her walking there a few weeks ago and decided to meet her. We both felt the need to talk and to get to know one another. I was supposed to meet her last night, but I have become apprehensive about everything that has happened, so I didn't go down. I guess Daniel saw her and met her in the gardens. Do you think the statue was meant for me? Allistair, I am afraid somebody is trying to scare me away or worse." Victoria moved closer and put her head on his shoulder.

"Sweetness, I need to figure out the next steps. Sorry, love, *we* need to figure out the next steps. I can't have anything happen to you." Allistair absentmindedly traced a heart on her left arm as he spoke.

"Let's go to dinner and act as normal as possible. I do not think we should let anyone know about the statue. We can meet back here later tonight to discuss everything. Then we can decide if anyone else needs to know the things that have happened aren't accidents."

She kissed his neck, and he quickly turned toward her and pulled her even closer. She was glad they were sitting because she knew her knees would buckle under his embrace. This kiss was the most passionate one they had shared so far.

Chapter Twenty-Six: A List of Suspects

VICTORIA had time to change and tell Emma to have a good night before she knocked on the panel leading to Allistair's room. In a few minutes, he entered her private quarters. She opened her arms as an invitation to come closer. They stood there for a few minutes before Allistair kissed her.

"Darling, things seem to be adding up that somebody is trying to scare me away. I won't allow my mind to think anything else is possible." She lied. She didn't want to admit her fears of the curse.

"Let's sit and discuss everything that has happened since you've been home." Allistair led her to the settee. "I made a list while waiting for you to knock on the panel," Allistair said, pulling out a piece of paper that he offered for her review.

Questionable Occurrences
1. Conflict with hired servant at birthday celebration.
2. Sighting at picnic.
3. Thrown in an open grave.
4. Stolen items.
5. Breaking of the buggy axle.
6. Sinking of the rowboat.
7. Thief coming through a secret panel.
8. Falling angel.

"Eight are eight too many. We need to try to figure out who is doing this and why," Allistair said, with a furrowed brow.

"On the mainland, I saw the same suspicious man three times after Sally's father threatened to find me. Now I have seen him here on the island. Maybe he is Sally's father, or there could be somebody here trying to make me return to London," said Victoria.

"No one has reported any strangers on the island since you saw the man at the lighthouse. That doesn't mean he's not hiding somewhere. Who on the island wants you to return to London?" asked Allistair. "The first person I thought of was Esther. She did try to throw you in the sea when you were a baby. Let's discuss why she could be the one or if we can remove her from the list."

"I immediately want to say she couldn't be the one, but I know we have to look at everyone," Victoria said.

"As I said, Esther tried to kill you once. Has she had the opportunity to do any of the eight items on our list?

As an old woman with cancer, Esther always has someone with her. Would she be able to saw an axle or drill a hole? She could have eluded her companion and gotten out of her rooms. Living here for so long, she would know where all the hidden passageways and panels are located. She could have taken your jewelry and other possessions, but that's the only one on the list I think she's capable of doing." Allistair looked at Victoria to see if she had anything to add concerning Esther.

"She couldn't have pushed the statue since she was in the gardens. Whoever pushed the angel had to do it when she and Daniel were exactly in the right place." Victoria was glad to take her off the list.

"Victoria, Esther has some people on the island who think she shouldn't be guarded anymore after all these years. Someone could be helping her try to scare you away. Her companion could even be on her side and helping with the things Esther can't do herself."

Allistair added a good point she had not thought about. Her heart sank at that revelation. She so hoped she and Esther would have the chance to continue building a relationship.

"Let's look at the next person. Your father does not have the strength to conduct most of the things on the list. He is the one who brought you home. Let's remove him. The next person to look at is Emma. She enjoyed her life in London and maybe wants to return. She could have done all the items on the list. What do you think?"

"Emma told me she enjoyed being in London but missed her family and was glad to be home. What about the axle? She almost fell off the buggy seat, and she was the one closest to the sea drop-off."

"Victoria, something happened when Emma and I were teenagers. You know we shared a tutor and were good friends while growing up. One day, unexpectedly, she said she had strong feelings for me. I did not want to hurt her but being a dumb teenager, I laughed when she declared her love. She stormed off and refused to come back to the manor after that. A couple of months later, Lord John offered her the chance to get an education in London. She left without even telling me goodbye. Maybe she still hates me for rejecting her and somehow knows about us?" Allistair kept his head down while telling her this story.

Victoria was surprised by the revelation, but the thought of Emma being guilty of any of these made her heart ache.

"We have been like sisters since she joined the Montgomery household. I cannot believe she never mentioned you but maybe being rejected was too hard to discuss with anyone. I talked about boys with her, but now that I think about it, she never mentioned anyone she liked romantically. Do you think she is trying to get back at you for rejecting her? I can't see her wanting to hurt me."

"Let's keep Emma on the list as someone to watch." Allistair looked at the paper again.

"How well do you know Henry?" Victoria asked Allistair.

"He is older than I by about eleven years and has lived

here his whole life except for five years in the Royal Navy. He was one of our best horse trainers but decided to travel the world. Henry could not be guilty of any of these; he returned a few days ago, and I know he wasn't the man at your birthday ball. Also, your items started disappearing a couple of weeks before Emma brought him to meet you. I cannot think of any reason he would want to frighten you either.

"Next is on the list is Daniel. He could have done all of the items except causing the falling statue to hit himself. He could have someone working with him, though. Maybe he thinks you will take away your father's love and his inheritance from him. Love and money are great motivators."

Victoria could see Allistair hated to even include Daniel as a suspect.

"I don't want to consider anyone on the island, but somebody is trying to scare or even harm me." Victoria's head ached. She reached up to massage her neck, hoping to release the pent-up stress. Allistair took over and gently helped the tight muscles relax.

"Let's stop for the night because my mind is spinning. I want you to be careful, Victoria. Why don't I hold you until you go to sleep?" He helped her rise from the settee. Allistair audibly inhaled when she removed her robe. For a minute, she reveled in the thought that him seeing her body even in a nightgown could affect him that way. She felt so cherished being cradled in his arms; she shut out the world, if only for a little while.

The next night, they met and considered anyone else

who might have made her a target.

"Allistair, your mother told me about your father's death and how she became depressed. She said she lived in a fog for many years and was not there for you. Do you think since you are close again that she is jealous of me? Maybe she wants me to leave, so you will continue to run all the operations on the island. Does she think you will be pushed out?" Victoria hated to ask these questions, but they had to look at every single one.

"She has had a difficult time, and I'm glad she seems to be returning to the land of the living. Thinking about your questions is hard, but she could feel this way." Allistair looked perplexed.

They eliminated the manor staff and island workers. They could not find any reason for one of them to want her to leave.

"The best thing to do is keep our eyes and ears open. I promise to always have someone with me. Maybe Daniel's near-death will make whoever is doing these things reconsider." Victoria tried to be optimistic.

"I do want to tell Daniel and your mother that these incidents are deliberate, not accidents. Do you agree?" Victoria asked.

"I'm sure you are correct that the person is probably scared now and won't continue, but we'll be diligent in keeping you safe. I will talk to my mother, and you can let Daniel know what we've found in researching each event.

"Let's think of good things now. I want to hold you each night. Does that suggestion meet your approval? Now, Ms. Montgomery-DuPree, I see the twinkle in your eyes. Nothing will happen that's not proper. I will control myself and you, too, until I make you, my Mrs. DuPree." Allistair laughed before pulling her close for one of his perfect kisses, using his tongue to explore the sweetness of her mouth.

This time, she returned his kiss using the tongue techniques he had taught her—techniques he had called French kissing.

Chapter Twenty~Seven: Every Rose has a Thorn

VICTORIA was glad Daniel didn't seem to have any ill effects and his arm had healed nicely, but the poor angel was beyond repair. A stonemason made a new one to replace the broken one.

Nothing else happened after the angel fell on Daniel two months ago. Whoever was trying to terrorize Victoria had apparently reconsidered or was afraid someone might die if the incidents continued.

Victoria could not help but tease Daniel about his feeling for Laura Wadsworth. He had not told Laura of his love yet, but Victoria thought he might say something at the yearly ball. Preparations for the house parties were ongoing on both islands.

"Daniel, I need to go to Swan Island to discuss the masquerade ball with Laura. Will you go with me?" she asked, knowing the answer would be yes.

"Laura could send one of her carrier pigeons, but with all the arrangements we need to discuss, they would fly their wings off, and I think she wants to see you, too." Victoria noticed Daniel turning red, but she did not want to embarrass him more.

"I'm glad it's a masquerade ball this year and that the Wadsworths are hosting it. I hope to learn from Laura all that I need to do for our turn as host next year. I have enjoyed working with her on the agenda, menus, activities, and entertainment," said Victoria.

"Sister, you will do an excellent job of planning next year's ball, and we will all help make your vision come true. The ferry that will bring our family and guests to the island will stop here first before heading to Swan Island. Each day, the ferry will go between islands according to which one is holding the activities. Everyone will return to the island where they are staying for dinner. On the day of the ball, we will relax until time to get ready to leave for the trip to the Wadsworths. It's exciting to watch the sunrise after a night of dancing, tasty food, and mischief on the ferry ride back."

Daniel seemed to enjoy Victoria's look of displeasure at how he said 'mischief.' Laughing, arm in arm, they headed to the beach to row across to Swan Island. Victoria was so glad that she had Daniel. They were the best of friends, and she tried to not think of how close she had come to losing him.

They rowed around to the beachside of Swan Island. Victoria knew that the ferry would dock there so everyone would have easier access to the manor than trying to climb the stone staircase on the island's cliffside.

Laura was waiting for them. Victoria had sent one of her pigeons back late yesterday with a note telling her when they would row over.

"Hello, Victoria," she said, grabbing her hand, pulling her toward the house. As if an afterthought, Laura turned back to Daniel and asked if he were coming as well. Victoria could tell he wondered why Laura seemed to be ignoring him. Apparently, they were more than friends, and probably love wasn't too far away.

"Laura, I've received RSVPs for everyone on my list. Both homes will be full to the brim."

"Only one family replied that they can't attend," Laura told her. "Everyone keeps mentioning how great the invitations look. You have such handsome handwriting. Cutting invitations in the shape of a mask and adding rhinestones and seed pearls around the eyes made them special. I think our clothing requirement for ballgowns and evening suits was a good idea." Laura talked a hundred miles a minute. Most of the time, Victoria let her do all the talking. She thought Daniel did the same.

"Let's finish the menu for the ball and start on the breakfast and lunch menus. Holding the daily activities and entertainment on a different island each day will make everything easier for us. We want to enjoy ourselves also." Laura turned back and gave Daniel a stunning smile. Victoria knew that helped his ruffled feathers.

He caught up to them and joined in the conversation. "I enjoy masquerade balls. Trying to guess other's identities is a great game. There are always some masked guests hoping to remain anonymous. This will add a humorous element to our ball since we're not wearing costumes. I know I will be excited when everyone reveals who they are at midnight." Daniel worked his way into the middle of Laura and Victoria. He linked arms with them as they gleefully walked the path to the manor.

When they had entered the parlor, Victoria deliberately took a side chair, leaving the settee for Laura and Daniel. She could not help but cover her grin with a small cough.

"Let's discuss ways to make this occasion as memorable as possible," Laura said, as Daniel inched closer to her.

"Every year since the house parties began, a couple has announced their engagement at the end of the ball. I wonder who the lucky couple will be this year."

Since Daniel knew about her and Allistair's secret engagement, Victoria thought he was talking about them. But looking over at Daniel, she saw he was smiling at Laura, who turned a lovely shade of pink.

"We will have a large breakfast and then serve tea between three and four o'clock. That will give everyone plenty of time to get ready. Does that sound to your liking?" Victoria looked for agreement.

"We will do the same on Swan Island," Laura said.

"On DuPree Island, tea will be set up in the dining room for the number of guests staying with us," Victoria continued. "This will also allow them to mingle throughout the early evening without having a set-in-stone time to arrive or leave. We'll use our finest China, sterling, and linens. Of course, Laura, since you are hosting the ball, you can do something less formal."

Nodding, Laura confirmed she was going to do that. "I don't want to add too much more to the list that the servants already have to do."

"Our menu will include tea sandwiches, cakes, scones, cookies, and assorted pastries, and of course, Devonshire cream. I want to include some of the popular foods grown on our island. We have fruit and berries not easily obtained on the mainland." Victoria had enjoyed trying the local fruits for breakfast and wanted to make them available for everyone partaking of the afternoon tea.

Daniel had been quiet thus far, but she knew he would have to speak up soon. He normally talked a lot, too.

"This is a good plan," Daniel said. "Tea will tide everyone over until dinner is served at the ball."

"Don't forget, when everyone arrives, there will be refreshments available, including drinks set up in the dining room. The refreshments will be simple: tea, lemonade, iced sherbet, ices, wafers, cakes, and bonbons." Victoria could feel her excitement growing. She would get to see the Montgomerys and find out more about her mother from the Stanfords. They had all replied with a confirmation that they would be coming and staying on DuPree Island.

"Here's the menu for the ball. Make any suggestions you think will add to a most spectacular night," Laura said. "I think we should have dinner at one o'clock after everyone has removed their masks." Laura passed Victoria a copy of the planned dinner menu.

After perusing the menu, Victoria only had a few suggestions. "Let's set up tables and chairs, including several large buffet tables on the lawn adjacent to the formal gardens with plenty of torches for light. Of course, we can have smaller tables inside for anyone who might not want to go outside."

Daniel took the menu from her. "Let me see the foods you have decided to serve. You know men enjoy a good spread."

The ladies rolled their eyes at him.

Daniel licked his lips and read aloud: "Cold meats; seafood dishes; white soup with rice; pea soup; many sweets including puddings made with fruit grown locally. Do not forget to have gin and whiskey. We have some of the best made on DuPree Island using our own wheat."

"Daniel, that's why I asked you to accompany me today. You know your food and drink, little brother."

Over the next few weeks, everyone had a list of things they needed to do for the masquerade ball. Victoria made two more trips to Swan Island. Allistair accompanied her once, and she really enjoyed that trip.

"Allistair, I adore having time alone with you."

"I am glad we have a few minutes at night to catch

up, and you know I look forward to kissing you goodnight. But being with you now, seeing the wind blowing your hair and sun upon your face, I can truthfully say I am happier than I have ever been." Allistair rowed effortlessly toward Swan Island. Victoria had seen his torso and knew his clothing hid how strong he was.

"Everyone has been busy. We will have twenty guests staying with us for two weeks. Martha and Emma are godsends. I know Martha was the lead for these house parties until Father asked me to take over. Do you think she minds?" Victoria did not want anyone to be angry with her.

"She hasn't said anything to me, and her demeanor hasn't changed either. Do not worry. I am sure everyone will like whatever you plan for next year."

At the Wadsworths' home, Allistair only joined the ladies for tea before excusing himself to talk to Laura's father, Sir Samuel, about his preparations for conveying guests to and from each island. He had some suggestions for preparing outside activities he wanted to discuss also.

When Allistair left the parlor, Laura leaned close. "Victoria, how long have you and Allistair been a couple?"

"Laura, how did you know? We want to wait to announce our engagement. Please don't tell anyone." She hoped no one else knew besides Daniel and now Laura.

"Let's finish discussing our plans for the ball. We only have three weeks. Time moves so fast," Victoria said, changing the topic.

They stayed for dinner and planned to leave before sunset to avoid having any problems rowing back home.

Sir Samuel wanted to show Victoria a new rose he had cultivated in the formal gardens. Everyone went out to see the rose he named "Laura."

"This is such a great tribute to your daughter. Have you always been interested in making new varieties of flowers?" Victoria asked.

"After moving to Swan Island, I looked for a hobby. This has turned into much more. I like creating." Sir Samuel bounced on his toes and tugged at his vest.

While the men discussed the different varieties of flowering shrubs, Sir Samuel had cultivated himself; Victoria inched along, inhaling the many fragrances that mingled. Laura excused herself to have a word with the cook.

The design of the formal gardens, with its hidden alcoves, or small benches for lingering and enjoying the beauty of nature, was magnificent. Scattered throughout were many statues waiting to be discovered.

"Do not move," somebody behind her whispered with a gruff voice.

Victoria froze.

"Do not turn around and do not say a word, or you will regret it."

"Who are you and what—"

A work-worn hand clamped tightly over Victoria's mouth, halting her questions. "I told you to keep quiet. You will listen, and I will tell you what I want."

Victoria reached up to try and pull the stranger's hand away, but he tightened his grip.

"Don't turn around, and I will not hurt you. Follow

my orders, if you know what is good for you," the man said, leaning in so close Victoria could feel his rank hot breath on her neck. "You need to leave DuPree Island and never come back, or someone you care about will be hurt. Are we clear?"

She nodded her head.

"I will be watching you. You either do as I have told you, or you will regret it."

Victoria could not stand to listen to him anymore. She raised her right leg and brought her foot down against his shin with as much strength as she could. Surprised by her action, he yelled, then grabbed his injured leg with the hand previously covering her mouth.

Victoria swung around, hoping to see his face, but he wore a homemade mask with holes cut for his eyes and mouth. It covered his whole head. She tried to remove it, but he grabbed her wrists. Angered by her actions, he slapped her face.

"You will regret hitting me," she said, refusing to cower before him.

The stranger laughed as if he were enjoying her suffering. He wrapped both hands around her neck and began to choke her. Trying to breathe and get away from him, Victoria realized escape was impossible as her world turned to blackness.

"Love," Allistair said, gently cradling her head on his lap. When she opened her eyes, Victoria could hear an immense sense of relief in his voice. "Please speak to me."

"My neck hurts," Victoria said, placing her hand on her throat as she tried to sit up. She thought she'd been dreaming when she heard Allistair's voice.

"Victoria, what happened? Why were you lying on the ground? You must have taken quite a spill. Let me help you stand. Do you hurt anywhere else?"

"The masked man must have placed me on the ground. He had his hands around my neck, choking me until I passed out."

"Who are you talking about?" Allistair asked.

Victoria told them what happened to her and that the mystery man said he would hurt someone she loved if she didn't return to London. A thorough search of the gardens turned up nothing. As everyone decided to go back inside, one of the gardeners ran up and handed a mask to Sir Samuel.

"That's the mask the man was wearing," Victoria exclaimed, touching her neck where red fingerprints were now visible. They would turn purple from bruising soon.

"We need to check the whole island. The rascal is here somewhere," said Sir Samuel. He and Allistair left to gather more men for the search.

The two ladies waited in the parlor. Laura sent a carrier pigeon to Daniel. "I informed him that you decided to spend the night here, and you will be home in the morning."

Waiting for any news was agonizing for the ladies. Finally, Sir Samuel and Allistair returned. Allistair quickly went to sit on the settee and hold Victoria's hand.

"We found the man's body. He seemed to have fallen from a cliff a few yards from our main beach. Tucked in a small cove, we found his boat hidden from sight. We think he followed you from DuPree Island and looked for his chance to attack you, Victoria," Sir Samuel said, slowly shaking his head.

"After checking his pockets, we found papers with the name *Frank Wallace* on them. Victoria, do you know that name?" Allistair asked her.

"No, I'm afraid I don't. Can I look at his face to see if he's the man that followed me from the mainland? I don't want to, but it would set my mind at ease if I could." Victoria shivered at the thought of seeing a dead person.

Allistair told her he was positive it was the scoundrel from the mainland, but he led her to the beach to see the man, knowing she needed to see for herself. Victoria inched toward the body. They had covered it with a tarp until his burial in the island cemetery.

"It's him! That is the man who followed me from the mainland." Victoria shrank back in horror at the injuries to his head. She quickly turned and hid her face against Allistair's coat.

Chapter Twenty-Eight: House Party

THREE WEEKS went by quickly as preparations for the house party were finalized. The anticipation was intense as everyone on DuPree Island waited for the ferry to arrive from the mainland. Victoria couldn't believe five months had passed since she had seen her adopted parents. She had mailed a letter to them every other week and shared many details about her life on the island. Victoria had not told them about the attacks. She did not want them to worry, and she was glad the danger was over. The person responsible was dead.

Victoria was extremely nervous about seeing her mother's family, Sir Benjamin and Lady Yolanda Stanford. Would they resent her being alive when Rebecca was not?

"Victoria, darling, we have missed you so much." Her

mother hugged her so tight that her father had to remind her to let Victoria breathe. He kissed her cheek and hugged her more gently.

"Mother, Father, I am so glad you are here. I cannot wait to introduce you to Lord John and everyone else. I want to show you the island. Everything is different but in a good way. How was your trip? We have so much to talk about."

Victoria looked past them and saw that her Stanford relatives were disembarking. Knowing now that Benjamin Stanford was Rebecca's brother, she could see the resemblance was unmistakable.

"Aunt Yolanda and Uncle Benjamin, I am glad you were able to come. I so look forward to hearing all about my mother, Rebecca." She hugged each with warmth. She was glad to have her birth mother's side of the family with her.

Getting everyone settled in their rooms was easy. Daniel's classmates were located on the east wing to minimize the noise of their late-night shenanigans. The other guests were in the west wing. Allistair did not have to change rooms, so he could come through the panel at night to discuss the successes and trials of each day.

The first day of the two-week house party started with a late breakfast to give everyone a chance to recover from their travels.

"Good morning, everyone. I hope you slept well. Did you find the schedule for each day's activities I left in your rooms?" Victoria moved around the crowd, greeting everyone.

"You have thought of everything. Our room is beautiful, and the schedule includes so many activities; how will we ever try them all?" Hannah was almost bouncing in her seat at the table.

Everyone expressed their joy of being house guests for two weeks. Some came every year, but there were quite a few who were first-time visitors. Renewal of old friendships and the creation of new ones warmed Victoria's heart. Each island took turns hosting the group every other day. On the first day, DuPree Island was the host. After breakfast, guests on Swan Island boarded the ferry for the other island. The first big event was lawn tennis. A special court was set up on DuPree Island for this popular sport. Women versus men and keeping score made the game more competitive.

"Some say lawn tennis is a lot of fun, but I say you should play the game as an excellent method of exercise and a useful mental outlet," said Uncle Benjamin, a short, portly man, heartily laughing and rubbing his belly. Everyone laughed along with him. He was a jovial man, always joking.

"Victoria and Laura, having an outdoor picnic on the beach is a great idea; the weather is perfect, the sea is calm, and no seagulls will rain down on us." Daniel laughed so hard at his lame joke he almost fell over a boulder near the boardwalk.

Everyone enjoyed more activities that afternoon before the guests from Swan Island traveled back for dinner.

The next day, the guests on DuPree Island boarded

the ferry to go to the other island. Croquet, an easy game played on a lawn, where the players hit wooden balls with a mallet through hoops embedded in the grass, was on the schedule as the main activity.

"I wish Lord John could have been with us today. He would have enjoyed seeing how competitive everyone was while playing croquet. I thought a couple of the women were going to hit Daniel with their mallets when he tried to cheat," Victoria said to her mother. She was enjoying her time with her family and getting to know the other guests.

Over the next two weeks, the agenda included equal time for relaxing, exploring the islands, walking on the beaches, or sitting in one of the gardens and talking with friends. Of course, Daniel and Laura's friends wanted to gather and relive memories from university and escapades they enjoyed in London.

Allistair and Sir Samuel organized activities for the men, including fishing, game hunting, horse racing, and a rowing competition scheduled for the day before the ball.

Both manors had an excellent billiard table where the men could play while enjoying their cigars and brandies after dinner. Finely tuned grand pianos in the drawing room were ready for musical performances each night after dinner. Any young lady wanting to show off her musical accomplishments at social gatherings and functions could play. Laura and Victoria knew that men eager to impress a woman would offer to turn her sheet music. This allowed the couples a few minutes to spend time together and flirt. Several ladies who were excellent singers added to the nightly entertainment.

She and Allistair even found time to sneak away. One night while the guests enjoyed music in the drawing room, they walked in the formal gardens.

"Will you join me for a walk in the gardens? My love, are you cold?" Allistair unbuttoned his coat and placed it upon her shoulders. The intimacy of the moment was exhilarating. Victoria leaned closer, parting her lips, inviting his kiss, which was beyond her wildest dreams.

"Darling, you drive me mad with desire," said Allistair.

Victoria drew in an impassioned breath when his hands cupped her breasts.

Something about being in a fragrant garden with moonlight illuminating the stone statues and putting their facial features in shadow, added to the intimacy.

Victoria relished getting to know Aunt Yolanda and Uncle Benjamin, especially the stories he told her of her mother.

"Rebecca was such a beautiful baby. She was slow to crawl because she knew one of her three older brothers would pick her up any time she reached out her arms. I laughed about her being a naughty schoolgirl, too. She was always getting into trouble with the teacher for pulling a pigtail or pinching a boy." Uncle Benjamin made a pinching motion with his fingers, and his cheeks turned ruddy. "All she had to do was giggle, and our parents couldn't spank her. She came to me when she fell in love with Lord John. She said she had met the man of her dreams and wanted my approval as her oldest brother."

Victoria cried but also laughed. Uncle Benjamin's stories made Rebecca more real to her.

Chapter Twenty-Nine: Not Really a Secret

AFTER DINNER one night, when Victoria was ready for bed, she knocked on the panel and waited for Allistair to join her. She got into bed, and when he entered, she motioned for him to accompany her. Together they rested side by side for a few minutes, not saying anything, just enjoying the comfort of knowing the person who loved you was there for you.

"Allistair, while you and the other men were fishing, Uncle Benjamin told me about my mother, Rebecca. His stories gave me a better idea of who she was as a person. In my mind's eye, I could see her clearly as he spoke. She and I were so alike growing up. As an adult, she had the same humanitarian passion as me," Victoria spoke in a soft voice.

"I want to do more for the youth on the island with

education," Victoria said, turning on her side to face Allistair. "We need to build a school for children ages six to fifteen and hire a teacher. I also want to start a scholarship for anyone over sixteen who wants to further their education by attending trade school on the mainland. The school and scholarship would be named in honor of Rebecca and help the children on the island. Do you think this is a reasonable goal? Will Father approve?"

"Sweetness, Lord John will approve of your wonderful idea. He will probably cry when you tell him about naming it after Rebecca." Allistair slipped his hand behind her back to play with her golden hair. He stroked her back all the way to the base of her spine.

"Victoria, I know how exhausted you are, and you have a busy day tomorrow with final preparations for the ball, but I want to ask you a question."

"You sound so serious. Should I be worried?" Victoria asked, trying to sit up, but Allistair wouldn't let her.

"Let's make our engagement official tomorrow night at the ball after everyone removes their masks. We can talk to Lord John in the morning. He told me he was going to have breakfast in his rooms. I also want us to tell my mother, Lord and Lady Montgomery, and the Stanfords.

"Since our family and friends are here, it's a perfect time. You have seen how much better Lord John is feeling. He has attended most activities here on DuPree Island but only as a spectator. To see him smile and clap for the winners has made my heart content. Resting tomorrow until time to get ready will be beneficial and give him renewed energy to go to Swan Island for the ball.

"He is determined to attempt one dance. He wants to waltz with you. The one before dinner, just before everyone removes their masks. While Laura is announcing the removal of the masks and that dinner will be at one o'clock in the morning, he can make his way to the dais to announce our engagement."

Victoria caressed his handsome face. "I love you, and yes, I want to announce our engagement at the ball. You are so sweet to want to tell Lord John and the others in the morning. They are family, and having them here together is a perfect time to make the announcement."

As they lay there, basking in their love, she snuggled closer and slowly drifted to sleep.

Victoria was running in her ballgown and mask as somebody was chasing her, trying to kill her. She was near the stone staircase on Swan Island, and the only way to safety was to quickly descend the steep steps to the beach below. Being so dark, only the first step of the staircase was visible. Her heart was beating so fast. She heard the sure footsteps of her assailant coming after her. She had to hurry. As she took the first step, she felt hands push her. She was falling, falling, falling.

Victoria heard someone screaming. She realized the sound was coming from her. Within seconds, Allistair was gently shaking her and telling her to wake up. Feeling safe with him beside her, she immediately went back to sleep without telling Allistair about the nightmare.

Victoria and Allistair entered Lord John's rooms while holding hands. They thought he had an idea that they were more than friends, but he had not said anything.

"Lord John, may I have your daughter's hand in marriage? We are in love and want to get married with your blessing." Allistair looked so handsome, standing in the sunlight coming through the windows. He was so strong and confident. Victoria knew Father could tell from their faces how much they cared for one another.

"My children, I am overjoyed for you. Allistair, you have my blessing to marry my daughter. Victoria, I have known for a while that you loved him. I knew something good was happening between you two. You have made my old heart so happy." Lord John grinned from ear to ear.

"Lord John—" Allistair started to talk, but Lord John raised his hand for him to stop.

"Allistair, after the announcement of your wedding is made, please call me Father. I have always thought of you as my son, and now you *will* be."

Allistair beamed. "Victoria and I hope you will agree to make the announcement tonight after everyone's masks are removed. We think revealing our engagement will be the perfect ending to the house party."

"I will be pleased to reveal such wonderful news tonight," Father said. "Victoria, save the waltz before dinner for me. I will only dance one time and want it to be with you. Removal of the masks event is the perfect time since we'll have everyone's attention. I will escort you to the dais and motion for Allistair to join us there." Lord John reached to give them both hugs.

Next, Allistair and Victoria found the Montgomerys coming from their room on their way downstairs. "Mother, Father, will you join us in Lord John's study for a few minutes before you go to the breakfast room?" Victoria asked.

They escorted them to the study and told them about the engagement.

"Of course, we will keep your secret. We are so delighted for you both. I saw you sharing special glances whenever you were in the same room. Victoria, you probably didn't realize it, but your last letter to us was all about Allistair. I told your father something was happening, and I would be overjoyed to hear the happy news. Allistair, thank you for loving our daughter." Mother dabbed at her eyes while Father shook Allistair's hand.

Victoria and Allistair next found Martha finishing her breakfast.

"Mother, I need you for a minute. It's about the ball tonight." Allistair steered her and Victoria into the library.

"Why? Did something else happen?" Martha went with them but remained noticeably quiet. Victoria hoped the news would help bring back Martha's enthusiasm and desire to be more involved in daily life.

"No, nothing has happened—well, nothing stressful,

that is. We have thrilling news. Victoria and I are engaged to be married." Allistair was holding his mother's hand and looked at her to see her reaction.

Martha gave them such a brilliant smile that brightened her whole face. Victoria had not seen her so animated. She hugged Victoria and Allistair both, then reached in her pocket for a tissue to wipe her eyes.

"Oh, this is good news indeed. I have felt there was something between you two," cooed Martha. "It's going to kill me, keeping this a secret, though."

The Stanfords were thrilled for them and said they thought they saw more than friendship blooming between them over the last two weeks.

Chapter Thirty: The Masquerade Ball

EVERYONE appreciated a day of relaxation and having plenty of time to get ready for the masquerade ball. Victoria couldn't forget the nightmare from the evening before. She believed she had manifested her fears through that dream.

Emma was excited about attending the function. "I have never been to the island's yearly ball. I was too young before I left for finishing school. Thank you again for my beautiful ballgown. I think Henry is more excited about the ball than I am. Father told me yesterday that Henry had been prancing around in his black suit and mask every night this week in anticipation of catching someone's eye. Just moments ago, he came to my room to show me how he looks and told me he was going to really enjoy tonight."

After Emma helped Victoria into her ballgown and secured her elaborate mask, she left to get ready herself.

Thirty minutes before they had to board the ferry, Victoria took another look at herself in the mirror and hoped Allistair would approve of her ballgown. She knocked on the hidden panel to let him know she was alone. He must have been standing there waiting because as she turned to sit on the settee, he opened the panel and entered.

"Fetching!" He reached for her hand and placed such a soft kiss upon it.

Victoria knew her ballgown was beautiful. The local island seamstress had designed the dress specifically for her. She had made all of Rebecca's clothes, so Victoria knew she was an expert. The seamstress was now training her granddaughter to take over when she retires.

Covered in rhinestones and beading with an iridescent ivory satin bodice and skirt, the ballgown fit her perfectly. The flounce was an exceptionally light blue, a pale version of the DuPree blue, lace-edged with tulle ruffles and decorated with embroidery. Victoria liked how her arms looked in the small lace cap sleeves. To ensure a proper fit and a touch of elegance, the seamstress used laces up the back with boning. The low décolletage showed just enough to not be improper and seemed to have commanded Allistair's attention. He leaned over and softly kissed the top of each full breast.

Victoria could feel herself blushing.

"I'm not sorry. I couldn't help myself even if I wanted to. You take my breath away, darling," he said.

"I have something special for you."

Allistair handed her a velvet box that contained the

most exquisite necklace and earrings. The jewels were the DuPree blue and reflected light with each movement. Victoria turned around so he could fasten the chain while she clipped on the earrings.

"Allistair, thank you." She kissed him with gratitude.

"My mother asked me to give you these. They are the pieces that my father gave her on their engagement night," he said.

Victoria admired how the jewelry paired impeccably with her ballgown as she looked at herself in the full-length mirror. She drank in Allistair's appearance also. His hair was well-combed except for the piece that always fell across his left eye. She felt such pride in the fact he would be hers soon.

"Allistair, you look dashing. I am so lucky to have you. We will have the best time tonight with all our friends and family members here with us. Soon everyone will know that we are in love."

The house guests met at the dock precisely at five o'clock. Victoria enjoyed listening to the ladies express wonder and surprise while comparing ballgowns. The elaborate masks, bejeweled and adorned with feathers, sparked the most conversation.

When her mother approached, Victoria exclaimed,

"Your satin gown is so pleasing. The color is perfect for you." Victoria always admired gowns trimmed in pearls and rosettes as this one was.

"Thank you, my dear." She kissed Victoria's cheek then motioned for Aunt Yolanda to join them. "Yolanda, your salmon-colored silk gown is a wonderful choice for you and makes you stand out," Mother said, as they boarded the ferry.

The sea was calm, so the trip to Swan Island was smooth. Victoria sat with Lord John. He looked fine, but she wanted to make sure.

"Father, I hope the motion of the ferry isn't making you sick."

"I can't feel ill tonight. My first trip off DuPree Island in two years is with my daughter, who looks like a princess. Martha told me she was giving Allistair her engagement jewelry as a special gift for you." Father brushed away a tear.

Disembarking, Laura and Samuel Wadsworth greeted them. "Welcome to everyone. We hope you will have a wonderful time tonight."

The formal gardens near the lake were in bloom as they strolled past statues and water fountains festooned with floral garlands. Lively music filtered through the doors opened to receive them. Joining the other guests in the manor foyer, Victoria noticed that Laura had concealed the entrance from the kitchen with flowering shrubs in clay pots and had woven evergreens on the staircase and throughout the gallery. She had obscured the fireplaces in each room with plants and flowers.

Emma touched Victoria's arm and whispered, "All the ladies are so attractive, and the gentlemen look dapper, wearing simple black masks with their black evening wear. Tomorrow my feet will kill me, but I plan to enjoy every dance."

Victoria giggled at Emma's enthusiasm. "I am going to enjoy the ball, too. Let's find the lady's cloakroom and leave our wraps."

Before going in, Victoria discreetly informed Emma, "If you need any help in arranging your hair or repairing torn clothing, the maids stationed here can help you. They also have hairpins, needles, thread, or just about anything a lady might need."

Greeted by many who hadn't seen him in a long while, Lord John was having a wonderful time.

"Victoria, I will make my way to the card room that is set up for those who do not want to dance. I want to get reacquainted with a few old friends. You go dance and enjoy yourself."

Victoria and Emma linked arms and entered the ballroom, ready to dance. Emma quietly told Victoria that two of her relatives who worked for the Wadsworths were responsible for the bright shine on the ballroom floor. . . . "Earlier in the week, they danced over and over on the floor. One wore brushes attached to his shoes, and the other wore soft cloths. They danced the waltz for four hours with a thirty-minute break between each hour. Laura gave them two days off to recover." As they tried to visualize how funny the men looked, they both laughed like old times.

Laura came gliding up to Victoria. "Trying to persuade the musicians to play all the popular music wasn't easy. But I did, and there will be eighteen musical arrangements tonight; eight quadrilles, six waltzes, two galops, and two polkas."

"Oh, great; Daniel lives to dance polkas," said Victoria, laughing at her own joke.

"Dinner will be served after the ninth dance. Do I need to make any changes?" Laura asked.

"Everything sounds perfect," Victoria said.

Seeing how well everything was going according to plan made Laura confident as she ordered the orchestra to begin. She took the lead in stepping to the center of the dance floor with her father, Sir Samuel. Daniel and Victoria were next, with other dancers following. Next year, with DuPree Island hosting the ball, Allistair and Victoria would be taking the lead. She looked forward to their future and all it would hold. Gentlemen and fashionably adorned ladies swirled about the dance floor. Some strolled around the room while others walked out on the terrace for fresh air.

"Laura, everything is magnificent. Thank you for your willingness to help with our announcement tonight. Your suggestion to have the staff pass out champagne to toast us will make the evening even more memorable," Victoria said, when passing her as she headed to the refreshment room.

Victoria noticed that Daniel couldn't keep his eyes from following Laura as she checked to see if anyone needed anything. Victoria decided to give him a little sisterly advice.

"Daniel," she whispered, "ask me to dance so we can talk."

As they danced, she glanced around the room, hearing the musicians but not seeing them since they were behind a bank of blooming flowers artfully raised in one corner of the ballroom.

"Dear brother, you resemble a puppy wanting your master to pet you. Ask Laura to dance already. I know she will accept," Victoria said, behind her ivory-feathered fan.

"Victoria, don't joke about it. I am seriously in love with her, but I'm afraid she doesn't feel the same. She has been ignoring me the last few days. I've seen her laughing with several of my university friends," Daniel sounded so disheartened.

"She's trying to make you jealous. When this dance is over, find her and ask her to join you on the floor. I know she won't say no," she said.

Victoria was surprised to see Martha dancing with Emma's father, Simon Jonas. Maybe she was looking for love again. Her relationship with him could be what Victoria sensed Martha was hiding.

Daniel finally took Victoria's advice and asked Laura to dance. Anyone watching them glide about could see it was apparent that a deep affection was growing between them.

Victoria observed Sir Samuel secure dancing partners for several ladies who appeared to be wallflowers. To not offend the self-esteem of the unfortunate ladies, he was discreet. The men, whom Sir Samuel requested to dance with these ladies, consented to his wish and even appeared pleased. Victoria was impressed by his concern for others' enjoyment. She hoped he would find someone to love again.

After dancing with several different partners, Allistair found Victoria on the terrace. "My love, may I have the honor of the next dance? You are without a doubt the most beautiful of all the ladies attending the ball."

As she placed one hand on his offered arm, she gathered the skirt of her soft blue gown in the other, and they moved toward the high columned entryway. In his arms and swirling around the floor was a dream.

"Did you notice your mother waltzing? She and Simon look good together, don't you think?" Victoria looked to see if he were upset to think his mother might find love again.

"I'm happy for her. Love makes everyone better people, and life is meant for love," he replied.

The waltz ended too soon.

A country dance with Daniel was next and so much fun. He was having an enjoyable time now that he knew Laura felt as he did.

"My lady, this is our turn." Lord John joined Victoria for the dinner waltz. They moved slowly because she wanted to make sure he did not overtire himself.

At the end of the last musical note, Laura stepped to the dais.

"Thank you all for attending the ball. Now is the time to reveal your true identities," she trilled.

"Everyone, please remove your masks."

She removed her mask, then everyone either untied or slipped off their own. Several people pretended to be stunned with whom they were dancing. Everyone laughed.

Laura clinked a glass to get everyone's attention. "Dinner will be served at one o'clock. Because we want you to enjoy the island's ambiance at night, tables are set up outside on the lawn under the enchanting stars. When the bell rings, please join us outside for dinner. Food will be buffet-style. Many of our local seafood delicacies, as well as a lot of typical English dishes, will be available."

Lord John and Victoria made their way around the crowd and stepped up on the dais.

Lord John shuffled forward. "Good evening, my friends. I have an important announcement to make. Allistair, would you please join us?"

Allistair stepped up on the dais beside Victoria.

"Everyone knows that my daughter, Victoria, has returned to her family here on the island. She now has two families. Lord and Lady Montgomery, would you join us, please. We're so delighted to have her home and that we get to share her with the Montgomery family. Martha DuPree, would you join us as well? I am so pleased to announce that Victoria and Allistair are engaged to be married." As everyone clapped and cheered, servants passed out champagne. "Join me in a toast. Here's to many, many, happy years."

Allistair knelt on one knee and opened a velvet box to reveal an exquisite opal ring surrounded by diamonds.

"Victoria, will you marry me?"

211

"Allistair, it will be my honor to be your wife."

He slipped the ring on her finger and kissed her as everyone cheered.

They stepped down from the dais, surrounded by many well-wishers. Allistair and Victoria couldn't help smiling from ear to ear, glad their love was now known by all.

Seeing Emma trying to maneuver through the crowd, Victoria wondered if she would be happy for them since she had loved Allistair when she was a teenager. Victoria had seen Emma dance with Steve Sims, and she seemed to enjoy his company. Maybe she had found love, too.

"Victoria, I'm so happy for you both," Emma said, hugging her. "I could see there was a connection between you and knew it wouldn't be long before an announcement would be made."

The band resumed playing, and the younger guests quickly went back to dancing. Soon a bell rang, signaling that dinner was ready. Sitting outside was so beautiful. Victoria loved hearing the cheerful voices of their families and friends as everyone enjoyed all the scrumptious food. Lord John moved inside when the night grew colder. Some of the men decided to play billiards, but other guests returned to the ballroom to enjoy a few more dances before the end of the ball.

Victoria heard Aunt Yolanda tell Laura that she had gone beyond all the requirements for a successful ball.

"Well done, my dear," she concluded, while many other guests congratulated Laura on hosting such an entertaining event. Several said they would never forget how delightful everything was tonight.

Chapter Thirty-One: The Killer Revealed

VICTORIA danced with several of Daniel's school friends, who were quite entertaining. "Victoria, marry me instead of Allistair. I will worship the ground you walk on. Wait, I will carry you, so you don't have to touch the ground. Will he do that for you?"

She didn't know how John Wiggington III could keep a straight face, but he did. She decided to let him down gently.

"My dear John, if only I had met you first, but alas, I have already agreed to marry Allistair. I'm sorry, but I know you will get over me soon. Probably in the next five minutes."

After a couple of seconds, they giggled so hard, they missed several steps of the dance.

Taking a break to catch her breath, Victoria was

sitting beside Lord John, who tapped his foot to the music as he watched the younger people move about in a lively country dance.

A servant approached Victoria. "Miss, I have a message for you."

He handed her a note from Allistair.

My darling, meet me on the bridge going over the lake. The one closest to the sea. I want us to celebrate privately, and I want to get a kiss under the stars. Your love

Victoria was excited that Allistair wanted her to meet him alone. Carrying her elaborate mask in her hand, she made her way down toward the bridge he said to take. She did not see him. Where was Allistair? When she reached the bottom, Victoria saw someone standing with his back to her a few yards ahead.

"Allistair, dear?"

She saw it was Henry when he turned toward her. "I am sorry, Henry. I thought you were Allistair. I received a note asking me to meet him here at the bridge."

"Allistair didn't ask you to come here. I did. The Royal Navy taught me how to forge handwriting. I did an excellent job convincing you Allistair wrote that note, didn't I?

"He's on the other side of the gazebo. I asked him to meet me there. I told him I knew who had been trying to scare you. When he arrived, I dumbfounded him by letting him know I was that person. I hit him with a large rock, taking advantage of his inability to wrap his head around my revelation.

"I'm sure he is dead." Henry smirked sinisterly.

"What?" Victoria felt the blood drain from her face. "No!" she cried, turning back toward the manor. A hand grabbed her arm and stopped her in mid-stride.

"Henry, let me go! I need to find Allistair."

"Why would you need to do that? I must talk to you without him interfering. And then you're going to die tonight." Henry's grip on her arm tightened.

"I will scream if you do not unhand me."

Victoria tried to appear brave, but she was shaking so much she was sure he could feel her vibrating.

"Scream all you want, the music's too loud, and now everyone's back inside, so it's futile."

Pulling her along, Henry mumbled to himself. "Why didn't you go back to London? If you had, none of this would have happened. I had everything planned, but you had to 'return from the dead.' Who knew that Allistair would fall for you?

"He was supposed to marry Emma. When they were teenagers, she told me that she loved him, but something happened, and she moved to London. Since Allistair was the assumed heir of Lord John, I would be set for life on the island if Emma had married him.

"When I completed my commission with the Royal Navy, I intended to return from the West Indies and have Emma come back to the island. Once Allistair saw her as a woman and not a school friend, he would have asked her to marry him. Eliminating Daniel would have been easy. Then Allistair would have inherited everything. I could've convinced my half-sister to give me everything I wanted. I could've taken over the horse training and made lots of money, betting on the ones we would sell for the Grand National. Training them would give me an advantage since I would know each one's temperament."

Henry had a look on his face as if he imagined all the money he would have.

Victoria knew getting Henry to talk would give her a chance to get away or for someone to find her. She decided not to mention 'eliminating Daniel' since she couldn't wrap her brain around losing her brother to a mad man.

"Let me go!"

She tried again to break free of Henry's grip, which worked this time.

Victoria ran as fast as she could, trying to get within hearing range of the manor. She began to yell at the top of her voice. But within seconds, Henry pulled her to a stop when he grabbed the back of her dress. She heard the seam down the back rip but not enough to completely give way. The sudden halt took away her breath, causing her to stop screaming.

"Yell out again, and I will cut your throat."

Seeing the blade of a large hunting knife, Victoria froze. She knew he had probably killed many while serving in the Royal Navy and would make good on his threat to use the knife on her.

"I won't scream again," she said, knowing she would if given a chance.

Henry started pulling her once again toward the cliff. When they were out of sight of the manor, he stopped.

"Do you want to know the whole story? You will go to your grave being the only one besides me who knows everything."

Victoria could tell that Henry wanted to gloat. She hoped if he did take time to talk, someone would rescue her.

"After my mother died, I found her diary," he continued. "She described in detail being raped by one of the deckhands from the ship that delivered goods to the island. She was only fourteen years old. The trauma for her and the disbelief for me as I read about her abuse was unimaginable. She soon found out she was having a baby. ME! I was that baby."

While Henry remembered the experience of finding out he was a child conceived by rape, Victoria dropped her mask, hoping someone seeing it would understand that she was in trouble and needed help. Thankfully, Henry didn't notice.

"My mother was friends with Simon Jonas and told him everything. He offered to marry her and raise me as his son. He said being friends made for a good marriage. She said 'yes' since her only other choice was to run away to the mainland. Becoming pregnant before being married is shameful for a woman. Simon kept his word, and I only found out I wasn't his son from reading the diary.

"When I was only a young child, my mother started showing signs of being mentally unwell. After having me, she suffered four miscarriages. That messed with her mind even more:—messed with her mind."

"Henry, I'm sorry about what happened to your mother. She would want you to let me go. I won't tell anyone." Victoria was willing to tell him anything to get him to release her.

"You know nothing about my mother; she was dealt an unfortunate hand from her youth. You are a spoiled rich man's daughter. Abandoned as a baby in London was traumatic for you, but now you have two rich daddies.

"Hold out your pampered little hands, and I'll cry you a river."

Victoria realized nothing she said would change Henry's mind about killing her. He got a faraway look in his eyes and became lost in his memories.

"When I was old enough to work in the fields with 'my father,' my mother became the manor's new cook. Before she started the job, she spent a couple of weeks with the retiring cook to learn how things worked in the kitchen. The old cook told my mother many stories about the DuPree family. Even some that should have gone with her to the grave. One was remarkably interesting—" He jerked back with a snarl. "*Baah*! You and your privileged life and all—you don't care about other people as you claim."

Henry shook his head as if slinging off a demon.

"I guess I'll just go ahead and throw you over the cliff.

That's what you deserve!"

Henry's mental state was deteriorating by the minute. Victoria needed to think of something fast, even if she had to lie to him.

"Oh, Henry. This was so unfair to you. Please continue telling me what your mother found out from the old cook." Victoria hoped she was convincing, but she really needed to stall him from throwing her off the cliff, if possible. She felt that time wasn't on her side.

Henry stood taller and his face beamed under the moonlight.

"You will be so shocked. I enjoy causing people to be shocked. *Nah*, the only shock I'll see on your face is when you fall to your death." He started pulling her faster.

"Henry, I bet you don't have more to add. You said your mother was having mental problems. So, she probably made up what was in her diary." Victoria was trying to distract him with another strategy. If she were successful, she could run toward the stone staircase. She knew a way to safely hide from him there.

Henry stopped and glared at Victoria.

"She didn't make up this story. Do not speak of my mother like that! I will end your life right here." He jabbed the knife inches from her throat, and she gave a muffled cry.

Maybe Victoria had gone too far, and he would kill her here and now.

"You almost got me," Henry laughed. "You can't break free again. I've got strong hands, unlike those pampered rich fellows you prefer. Now, where was I in the story?

"When your grandmother was pregnant with Karen, the cook prepared many dishes for her to eat, but nothing agreed with her. Rice pudding was the only food that she could eat without throwing up. Eventually, the old cook figured out one spice was helping with the nausea.

"Do you know which spice is used in rice pudding? I'll tell you. Using too much nutmeg can cause intoxication, but they didn't know that back then. Esther had anxiety, confusion, and dizziness. All things that happen when you're pregnant. She continued to eat nutmeg on everything even after giving birth. The old cook thought she was helping the mistress of the manor to feel better." Henry gave a gleeful laugh.

"Are you saying Esther was drugged when she threw Karen into the sea? She didn't know what she was doing?" Victoria's mind was numb from all he was telling her.

"She overdosed and began to hallucinate. She told her maid that the sea always soothed her when she was upset, and since the baby would not stop crying, she took Karen with her. She kept muttering to herself, 'I had to throw the bucket of water into the sea' on the way back to the manor.

"After she threw Karen into the sea, everyone thought Esther had lost her mind. Her husband never spoke to her again. Victoria, imagine your life if anyone had known about overdosing on nutmeg? I guess we'll never know how different things would have been. Too bad." Henry laughed again.

"Do you know why Esther tried to throw me into the

sea? She had to be mentally imbalanced. Right?" She kept cutting her eyes toward the horizon, hoping someone would be out walking and see her.

"Simon Jonas always wanted a daughter, so my mother kept getting pregnant to please him. She was jealous that Lord John and Rebecca had just had a daughter. My mother saw you as an enemy and sent from the devil.

"Using the information learned from the old cook, my mother drugged your grandmother with nutmeg again, knowing how the spice would affect her. She added the nutmeg to all her food. She even mixed some in her wine. To make sure, before Esther tried to throw you from the cliff, my mother would spend time with her each day and always mentioned how comforting the sea was when she was upset. In Esther's state of mind, the thought took hold, and she once again went to the cliffside where she tried to throw you into the sea. Before my mother died, she confessed to me what she had done to try to kill you. I was only twelve years old. I didn't know what she wanted me to say or do at her revelation. But now I understand why she did it.

"You are evil!" Henry spit out the words.

"I think it's funny that nutmeg comes from the West Indies and that I spent the last few years there while serving in the Royal Navy." Henry's eyes glazed over with memories. "My mother often talked about her dream of me one day owning the island and all its riches. With the thwarting of your drowning and then miscarrying for the fifth time, she could not face life anymore. She committed suicide. I found her body in her bedroom with a bottle of laudanum beside her.

"I knew you were responsible for her death and was glad that you 'died' on the voyage home from the mainland all those years ago."

Keeping quiet so he would continue to talk, Victoria felt sorry for a young boy finding his mother dead but not for the man now holding her hostage. She had to try one more time to escape. Henry was facing her now and was at the perfect angle for him to feel the impact of her shoe hitting his private parts.

After earlier attempts made on her life, Allistair taught her how to kick for optimum effect. With dresses being different for each time of the day, he made sure she could kick no matter the type of dress she wore. They had even practiced with her wearing a ballgown.

When Henry pulled the back of her dress, he didn't know he had caused a rip that had spread downward, giving her even more room to get momentum for the kick. Slowly Victoria moved her right leg back under her skirt, aimed as high as possible, and with her foot, she made direct contact.

Henry yelped and doubled over. His hand at once went to his groin.

Running as fast as she could, Victoria almost reached the top of the hill leading to the manor before Henry caught her again. How had he recovered so quickly?

Victoria's hair had escaped its elaborate updo and was streaming down her back. Henry started dragging her backward by it. The pain was excruciating, and she was sure some of her hair had been pulled out by the roots. He must've known she had to concentrate on not tripping and wouldn't have time to try to escape again.

She was glad that Henry had only one thing on his mind: Trying to throw her off the cliff. With his right arm extended behind his back, causing his dinner jacket to stretch open, he didn't notice the knife he put in his breast pocket fall out. Victoria was thankful he would not be able to threaten her with it again.

Finally, Henry stopped dragging her and turned her around.

He gave a scary high-pitched laugh.

"Victoria, dear Victoria. I tried to scare you away, but that didn't work. I hired a friend of mine to follow you from the mainland. He made sure you saw him at your birthday celebration, the coaching inn, and the lighthouse on DuPree Island. He was also the one in the gardens here on Swan Island. I was hiding in the boat, waiting for him to come back after scaring you, and a brilliant plan came to me. I pushed him to his death so you would believe you were finally safe.

"My mother told me about a secret panel that she accidentally found while working in the manor. I sometimes went with her to work on Saturdays, which gave me time to explore. I found several panels that let you quickly move around the old place. They also allowed you to hear conversations that others think are secret.

"I was the one who took your jewelry and other items. I learned a lot from reading your letters to the Montgomerys. I saw you when you found out they weren't in date order. You thought you did that," said Henry. "I enjoyed seeing you asleep in your bed when I came into your room through the hidden panel. I should have stolen a kiss from you before Allistair got the chance."

Victoria stiffened. Had he been spying on their most intimate moments? She kept looking around to see if there was anything that she could use to aid her escape from this madman.

"Cutting the buggy axle should have caused your death, but having Emma with you on the seat balanced the buggy just right."

"But weren't you concerned about your sister, Emma? Don't you care about her?"

"*Nah*, I wouldn't have been upset if Emma had died, but neither one of you were even scratched. I thought for sure you wouldn't survive the boat sinking. I heard you mumbling to yourself about going rowing and knew that would be the best way to get rid of you. I told Emma I had to go to the stables, but instead, I quickly went to the kitchen, stole some brown sugar, took a drill from the stables, and headed to the beach. Luck was with me that no one was in sight. I quickly drilled a hole in the first rowboat and filled it with brown sugar. Being you were distraught, I felt you would take the first rowboat, which you did. I was sure that no one would hear you scream as the boat sank. But from the hillside, I saw your rescue.

"I laughed so hard when the next idea to eliminate you came to me. You are a devil who is ruining my dreams for my future so using an angel to kill you seemed the right choice. The stone statue should have finished you in the garden, but you decided not to meet your grandmother that night, and instead, the angel hit Daniel. I thought for sure you would be afraid that someone else in your family would be hurt or worse if you didn't go back to London. But you didn't leave.

"When my friend assaulted you here in the formal gardens, I thought for sure you would leave. I told him to do whatever he thought would terrorize you. When he said he choked you until you blacked out, I congratulated him just before I pushed him from the cliff to his death.

"Victoria, this is the last time someone will say your name. Do you hear Hell calling you? The time for talking is up. So are your attempts to break free."

Henry pulled Victoria the last few feet to the edge of the cliff. The stone steps were inches from their feet, and the sea breeze had intensified.

Chapter Thirty-Two: Twinkling Rhinestones

ALLISTAIR slowly turned over. With every move, pain shot through his head. "Where am I? Why is my head hurting?" He carefully reached behind his throbbing right ear. When he withdrew his hand, warm and sticky blood was all over his fingers. Somebody hit him with something hard enough to split the skin and knock him unconscious, he realized. Fear gripped him to his inner core as he remembered everything that had happened.

Carefully he sat up and staggered to his feet. Moving as fast as he could toward the manor, Allistair knew time was against him. Victoria was in trouble. When he entered the ballroom, Daniel saw him and hurried to his side.

"Allistair, why is your suit stained and your hair so disheveled?" When he saw the blood on Allistair's hand, his eyes enlarged. He tried to shield Allistair from the other guests in the room.

With urgency in his voice, Allistair gripped Daniel's arm with the hand not covered in blood. "Have you seen Victoria? I need to find her. Henry hit me over the head and knocked me out but not before telling me he is the one trying to kill her. He said he would accomplish that tonight."

"Oh my God! She was sitting with Father a few minutes ago. Go to Sir Samuel's study, and I will ask Father if he knows anything. I will then meet you there with several of my friends, and we'll search every inch of this island." Daniel seemed so calm, but Allistair could see the fear in his eyes.

Waiting in the study for Daniel seemed a lifetime. Allistair picked up the brandy decanter and sloshed a generous amount in a glass. He gulped it down and paced while thinking that his future bride was somewhere breathing her last breath. Allistair was determined to go look for her by himself if necessary.

As he reached for the doorknob, Daniel swept in with three of his friends.

"Father said a servant handed Victoria a note about ten minutes ago. She told him she was going to meet you to look at the stars. We now know the note wasn't from you. Let's split up and search the whole island."

Daniel and one friend were going to search the beach and ferry. The other two friends would search the manor while Allistair would head toward the cliff and stone staircase.

Running toward the bridge leading to the cliff,

Allistair was afraid that none of them would reach Victoria in time. He could see no one was near the manor side of the lake. He quickly crossed the bridge, trying not to make too much noise. He didn't want to let Henry know someone was coming his way if he stumbled upon him.

When he reached the bottom of the bridge, neither Henry nor Victoria was anywhere in sight. Allistair ran up the hill, but he couldn't see any movement in the darkness down below. As he turned around and headed back to the manor, the moon's glow through the trees reflected on something lying on the grass to his right. He walked over to see what it was and could only gasp. Victoria's mask! Thank goodness she added more rhinestones around the eyeholes yesterday. They were the reason he saw the mask. He was in the perfect spot to see the rhinestones twinkling in the moonlight.

Allistair knew she and Henry had come this way. He wouldn't have time to go back and alert anyone else, so he moved as fast as possible toward the cliffside. Henry was either going to take Victoria down the staircase or, worse, throw her from the top of the cliff.

There they were, up ahead. Allistair saw Victoria struggling to break free.

Inwardly, he was furious, but he kept calm, the rage well-hidden. He needed to distract Henry and give Victoria a chance to run away.

"Henry, stop right there!" he yelled, as loud as he could.

Henry stiffened, then turned around and saw Allistair. He looked back at Victoria and released her as if knowing she had nowhere to hide from him. Henry then headed in Allistair's direction, breathing hard through an open mouth.

"Well, Allistair has come back from the 'dead,' too. I thought I hit you hard enough to kill you. Have you come to see your bride-to-be fall to her death?" Henry walked with determined steps.

"You will not harm anyone else tonight. I will make sure of that." Allistair knew Henry was fit from being in the Royal Navy, but he, himself, was in good shape from working with horses every day. He knew he could take Henry this time since the bastard had shown his hand at the gazebo.

Allistair circled Henry, trying to buy Victoria time to escape. He looked her way for a second. He saw her run toward the stone staircase instead of away from it. What was she thinking? He prayed she wouldn't try to go down the stairs. It's too dangerous with only sporadic moonlight.

"When *exactly* did you arrive back on DuPree Island?" Allistair asked.

"Why do you ask? Oh, I understand. You didn't think the villain could be me trying to scare Victoria away since I wasn't *here* when the first incident happened. I hired a friend, Frank, to scare Victoria, but once he had done what I needed him to do, I took care of him on Swan Island. I wanted to give you a false sense of security.

"I tried the 'Is Victoria Crazy' stage of my plan. You don't know, but I'm very familiar with the hidden passageways inside the manor. I was able to hide inside them for a couple of weeks. My, you sure don't know how to make love to a woman. Domination of women is a man's goal. Take what you want, even if the woman says no. They like to play hard to get." Henry licked his lips as if he were remembering taking what he wanted from women before.

Allistair needed to control his temper until he could make his move, so he gritted his teeth and clenched his fists. He ducked his head and ran at Henry, hitting him in the chest, knocking him down. As he tried to pass the prone body, Allistair felt a hand grab his leg, causing him to trip and hit the ground hard on his right knee. Before he could move, Henry was on top of him, punching wherever he could reach.

Somehow, Allistair got in a punch. The sound of bones breaking with blood spewing everywhere had Henry reaching for his nose. Allistair was able to throw him off and sprang to his feet, but not fast enough. Henry hit Allistair's right knee so hard, he couldn't catch his breath until the moment he screamed when his damaged knee crashed on an exposed rock. Allistair couldn't get up from the dew-dampened ground, giving Henry a chance to run after Victoria.

"Victoria, hide. Henry is coming!" Allistair yelled, trying to get to his feet.

Chapter Thirty-Three: Upstairs, Downstairs

VICTORIA saw Allistair coming toward them and became hopeful. When he yelled at Henry, she used that opportunity to pull away. Henry turned from her and walked toward Allistair. She knew she must get away quickly. Running parallel to the cliff was the logical solution, but Henry would be able to catch her. Thank goodness he had dropped the knife. He wouldn't be able to pull the blade on Allistair or her now.

Victoria took the stone staircase. Twice she and Daniel had used the stairs when visiting Laura to discuss preparations for the ball. He showed her which steps were the most dangerous and how to safely traverse them.

The stone carvers cut two steps deeper because of the change in the cliff's direction, creating a crevice where she might be able to hide. The first one was four steps below the ridge. Victoria safely got to that one and moved as far back into the recess as possible. Because it was still dark and the morning sun had not broken the horizon, maybe if Henry came down the steps, he wouldn't see her there.

She heard Allistair yell that Henry was coming. She was glad the crash of the sea covered the sound of her breathing.

"Victoria, you can't hide.

"I'm coming to get you.

"You have to die,"

Henry sang as he started down the stairs.

He reached the step where Victoria was hiding but continued onward without stopping. She hoped he thought she had reached the beach below where he would be able to capture her easily since there's nowhere to hide down there.

When Henry reached the sixth step, Allistair yelled at him from the top.

"I will stop you. You will not harm Victoria."

Henry laughed hysterically.

"I will reach her first, then I will take care of you."

Allistair got to the third step and stopped. She heard him moan. Was he injured? He limped as he moved past her. He didn't see her hiding on the fourth step either. She didn't want to startle him, so she kept quiet. He got to the fifth step and yelled again.

"Stop, Henry!"

The wind blew the clouds away, and the full moon shone brightly upon the steps. Victoria moved out enough to look down. Henry had reached the eighth step. That was the most dangerous step, Daniel had stressed. And one could easily lose their balance on it.

Henry took another step, teetered, then began falling but not straight down to the beach. The staircase curved back the other way, so he hit the sides of the cliff most of the way down. Under the moonlight, only the white dress shirt under his coat was visible as he fell to the lower depths, screaming.

Victoria screeched and hid her face. She knew there was no way Henry could have survived a fall from that height. Within seconds, Allistair found her.

"Darling, I have you now."

Chapter Thirty-Four: Solemn Ending

ALLISTAIR gave Victoria his jacket since she was shaking so hard. He helped her to sit down on the stone step where she had been hiding in the crevice.

"Sweetheart, I need to go down to the beach to check on . . . . Will you be okay until I return?"

"Yes. Please be careful on the eighth step." Nothing else would get past the lump in her throat. She knew she was traumatized, but she couldn't feel sad for Henry. He was going to kill her and Allistair.

"Victoria!" She heard Daniel yell from above.

"Daniel, I am on the fourth step. Be careful coming down," she called back.

He and two of his university friends carefully made their way down to her. Daniel lifted her and hugged her tightly. Victoria informed them that Henry fell to the bottom, and Allistair had gone down to check on the situation.

While one of Daniel's friends helped her back up to the top of the cliff, he and the other friend continued down to assist Allistair.

In a few minutes, everyone was back on the top of the cliff. Allistair held Victoria close as they walked back to the manor.

"Allistair, why are you limping? Is your leg hurt?" Victoria asked, wondering if he had been wounded from his fight with Henry?

"I'm all right. My knee is a little sore from falling on a rock," Allistair replied.

Sir Samuel and Laura met them at the top of the bridge holding lanterns.

"What has happened?" demanded Sir Samuel. "We saw two of Daniel's friends going from room to room, searching frantically. When I asked for an explanation, they said Henry Jonas had knocked Allistair out and had abducted Victoria. They told us where the rest of you were searching. Daniel returned from the ferry without finding you, so we knew the stone staircase had to be where you were."

"Henry tried to kill Victoria, and, in the process, he fell from the stone staircase to the rocky beach," Allistair said. "I will never forget the look of death on Henry's face. He was impaled on a sharp rock just inches from the last step."

"Victoria, come with me. The men will take care of everything." Laura led her inside.

Before the door closed, she heard Sir Samuel tell two men to row around to the cliffside beach and bring back Henry's body. Victoria was glad her parents didn't know about her abduction until she returned safely.

"Laura, please take me to my parents."

Lord John was the first one they saw in the ballroom. When he saw her face, he knew something had happened. Standing, he pulled her close as she burst into tears. The Montgomerys saw her overcome by her emotions and rushed over. She moved into her mother's arms while both of her fathers encircled her with love.

Allistair arrived in the ballroom while Emma worked her way through the crowded dance floor to see if she could help with whatever was upsetting Victoria. Oh, how would they be able to tell Emma about her brother? Victoria knew she wouldn't be able to say any kind words about Henry.

"Allistair, please tell Emma about Henry falling to his death. I think you should save all the details for later after she has had time to realize he wasn't who she thought he was." Victoria clung to his arm.

"Darling, I will be as gentle as possible and not tell her the whole story until we are back on DuPree Island," Allistair said, turning toward Emma when she finally reached them.

He pulled her aside and explained that Henry fell to his death.

Emma collapsed.

Steve Sims, DuPree Island's farm manager, caught her before she hit the floor.

"Daniel, find Dr. Williams; he's here somewhere with his wife, Penelope. He always has his medical bag with him," said Victoria.

Dr. Williams gave Emma something to calm her nerves. When others in the ballroom started asking questions, Sir Samuel decided to make an announcement.

"May I have your attention? There has been an accident with someone falling from the stone staircase. We need to end the night with everyone from DuPree Island going to the beach and boarding the ferry for the return trip. Those staying here on Swan Island, if you would please, go to your rooms."

Allistair stayed behind to help. Before Victoria left the ballroom, he kissed her cheek.

"I love you, Victoria. I am so sorry that I couldn't keep you from such an evil person. I will be home soon. Let the family take care of you until I return," he whispered in her ear.

With Simon Jonas on one side and Steve Sims on the other, they supported Emma as they walked to the beach for the trip home. Daniel helped Father navigate the beach while quietly giving him more details. Martha and the Montgomerys were in a state of disbelief. No one talked on the trip back to DuPree Island.

Victoria watched the ferry sail away on the return trip to

Swan Island to pick up Henry's body. She wanted to wait for its return because Allistair would be on the ferry, too.

Daniel found her shivering on the beach and persuaded her to come inside. "Everyone is gathered in the parlor, waiting for the doctor to let us know how Emma is doing," Daniel said.

Steve Sims would not stop pacing nor take a seat. "I can't rest until I know about Emma," he said.

Victoria had noticed earlier at the ball, Steve danced with Emma several times, making her think a budding romance was taking place. He had been so helpful in getting her back to the manor. Victoria hoped Emma would draw strength from him during this difficult time.

"She has been sedated and put to bed; sleep is the best thing for Emma. She should be out for twelve hours. Her mind needs the rest," Dr. Williams said to Martha. "Check on her a couple of times tonight, and I'll be back in the morning."

Victoria encouraged the Stanfords to go to their room while Daniel helped Father to his rooms. "I'll come up in a few minutes," Victoria said.

After Father left the drawing room, the Montgomerys looked at Victoria with more concern than they had while Lord John was in the room. She thought they were so kind to think of his health and wanting to keep him stress-free.

"Victoria, should we be worried about you? We can stay with you if you want."

Mother looked ready to cry at any minute. Victoria embraced her. "I will be all right. Please don't worry too much." Reluctantly they left to go to their room.

Martha convinced Victoria to allow her to help change her clothes. Later Martha went to make tea, and Victoria headed to Lord John's rooms.

"Father, I promise I will tell you the whole story tomorrow." Tucking him in, she was able to reassure him. His manservant had his medicines ready.

Returning to the drawing room to wait for Allistair, Victoria found that Martha had encouraged Steve Sims to go home. "I told Steve I would send a message to let him know as soon as Emma wakes up. The poor man really fancies her and will worry until he sees her himself."

"Martha, I am so glad you are my friend. Your strength is so helpful."

"I'm happy you will be my daughter. I will always be here for both of you."

"Martha, I saw you dancing with Simon Jonas several times. Have you had time to talk to him about Henry? I know everything happened so quickly."

"He's with Emma now, but we did speak for a minute. I told him I was available any time he wanted to talk. He is a strong silent man, but tears shone in his eyes when Allistair pulled us from the dance floor to let us know about Henry's death and Emma fainting. I will take Simon tea when Allistair arrives home and can be with you," Martha said, with an unsteady voice.

The door opened, and Allistair limped inside the room. He looked so exhausted. Opening his arms, he pulled Victoria into a tight embrace. Comforting each other, they never heard Martha leave the room.

Chapter Thirty-Five: Not Guilty

VICTORIA heard heavy footsteps coming nearer and knew Henry was looking for her. Hiding in a cleft in one of the steps, she hoped to make him think she was on the beach below. Suddenly, he was standing on the fourth stone step, her hiding place. Before moving to the next step, Henry giggled to himself then rubbed his hands together. He turned around, bent over, and glared at her. A clammy sweat broke out over Victoria's whole body, and her teeth chattered. Henry roared with laughter as he reached for her. She wailed into her hand. Victoria struggled to get out of his rough grip by hitting and kicking. She even tried to bite his arms as they reached to pull her from her hiding place.

"Victoria, you are having a nightmare. Wake up, darling." Allistair tried to soothe her, but the dream seemed so real.

241

After a couple of minutes, she was calm enough to understand she was in her bed at the manor, and Allistair was the one holding her.

"The dream was so real. Is Henry really gone? Is he dead?" Victoria asked, still feverish and unsettled from the whole experience.

Over the next couple of days, guests departed for their homes on the mainland. The end to the house party wasn't as expected, but everyone expressed how they would gladly accept an invitation to come back next year.

Victoria had another nightmare before Henry's funeral. Her experience on the stone staircase affected her more than she let anyone know. Not fooled by her upbeat attitude, Allistair kept a close eye on her. She ran around, helping everyone prepare for their return trip, hardly stopping to rest. He finally asked her to meet him in her rooms.

"Victoria, we need to talk. You are almost at your breaking point. I know you had another nightmare last night, and you hardly touched your food today."

"Allistair, I feel responsible for causing Henry's death and ruining the house party. Because of me, Emma is distraught and almost died in the buggy incident. I don't want to leave you, but maybe I should move back to

London," she said, feeling so guilty. "I didn't tell you, but I overheard one of the guests at the ball gossiping. She said that the island hadn't had all this turmoil until I returned and that perhaps the sea god legend was true after all."

"I need you to stay, but if you feel you should leave, I will go with you. You are not cursed or responsible for any of the things that happened. Henry was mentally imbalanced, and his death was because of that and nothing more," Allistair said, hugging her from behind.

Knowing Allistair would leave the island he loved for her meant more than any words could. She listened to his concerns and realized he was right. Still feeling melancholy at times, she slowed down, and her appetite returned. She found that talking with others helped diminish her feelings of guilt and reminded her how much her family cared about her.

Everyone on both islands attended Henry's funeral, not because of any affection for him but to support Emma and her father. Martha worked with the cook to make sure Emma and Simon had all the food they needed.

"We should be there for them. Everyone who knew Henry can't believe he wasn't who they thought he was. The revelations about his life and his sinister plans have left us all dazed."

Everyone agreed with Martha and helped in any way they could. Allistair found Henry's hiding place in the secret passageways. He had supplies and could have stayed hidden in the passageways for a month more, at least.

"I found his mother's diary, and it confirmed everything. Emma's father, Simon Jonas, had other documents his first wife wrote that matched the handwriting. The yellowed pages and the faded ink showed the diary's age. So, we know Henry didn't forge any of it. I also found a diary in the hidden passageways that Henry used to write about his plan to scare Victoria away. When that didn't work, he became obsessed with killing her," Allistair announced at dinner.

"I think both diaries should be given to Emma and her father," Victoria said to Allistair, later that night in her bedroom. They might not want to read them now, but I hope they eventually do. I understand Emma needed to move home with her father, but I wish she would let me see her. At least the diaries will provide proof that I didn't make up the stories Henry told me. I hope it will help repair my friendship with her."

Allistair agreed and delivered the diaries the next day to Simon.

Emma wouldn't talk to Victoria for a month, but after dealing with her grief and then disbelief, she asked Victoria to come to her father's home. When the door opened, Emma was crying.

"Victoria, can you ever forgive me? Henry was inclined to brood and sink into lengthy periods of silence, but I never thought he would try to kill anyone, especially my best friend." Her apology came out between sobs that racked her much slimmer frame.

"You don't owe me an apology. Henry was the one behind all the attacks and such," Victoria said, holding Emma tightly. "Our friendship is too strong for his crimes to separate us."

After finding that the diary proved Esther wasn't responsible for Karen's death or trying to kill Victoria, Father called a family meeting.

"Daniel, please bring your grandmother here. This is a family meeting after all," he said, smiling at everyone who gathered in the parlor.

When Esther entered the room that she hadn't been in for over twenty years, Father started to cry. Grandmother stepped toward him but stopped, not sure whether she should go to him or not.

"Mother," he said, with a trembling chin. "I have missed you so much." He slowly got up from his chair and took her hands. He looked at Allistair to explain everything.

"Lady Esther, . . . we have proof that you were drugged when Karen was thrown into the sea and then again when Victoria was almost drowned. You are not guilty of any wrongdoings." Allistair seemed happy to give her this news.

Everyone could see the shock on Grandmother's face, which paled at this revelation. She reached out to hold on to Daniel, who was still standing beside her. Her eyes darted from Lord John to Allistair as if to confirm it wasn't a bunch of buffoonery. Seeing her unsteadiness, Daniel led her to the settee to sit beside Victoria, who put her arm around Esther's shoulders.

"You mean, after all this time . . . I'm not responsible for killing my baby or trying to kill you, Victoria?" Hope brightened her countenance.

"Grandmother, someone drugged you both times," said Victoria. "You didn't know what you were doing."

"You mean my poor William went to his grave, thinking I was a murderer?" she silently cried.

Victoria moved over, so Father could sit beside Esther and offer words of comfort.

Chapter Thirty-Six: Love is in the Air

OVER THE NEXT few months, Emma Jonas and Steve Sims grew closer. They announced their engagement one night after dinner. The next day, Emma came to the manor to discuss wedding preparations.

"Victoria, will you be my maid of honor?" Emma asked.

"Yes, my dear friend, I would be honored to be your maid of honor." Victoria giggled.

Emma and Steve didn't want to wait to be together, so they were married within two weeks at the manor. The reception was in the formal gardens, and everyone danced the night away in the ballroom.

Daniel and Laura were inseparable. They sent carrier pigeon notes to one another at least two times a week, and Daniel rowed over to Swan Island whenever possible to see her. Naturally, everyone expected an announcement from them as well.

Allistair and Victoria began preparations for their wedding. A month before the happy occasion, Victoria personally penned invitations to family and friends on smooth white paper, using calligraphy to add a romantic touch.

The morning of the wedding dawned bright with calm weather. Those attending the ceremony had arrived two days ago and were either staying on DuPree or Swan Island.

Victoria awoke alone because Allistair slept in his old room last night. He grumbled about it, but she insisted because it was bad luck for the groom to see the bride before the wedding. She looked forward to him becoming her husband in just a few hours.

"Victoria, you look so angelic. Rebecca's wedding dress is lovely on you. Hannah was touched when you asked to wear her wedding veil. The tiara of orange blossoms will look lovely on your golden curls. Honoring both of your mothers will only make your wedding more special." Emma beamed, while adjusting the dress's train.

"Thank you, Emma. My mother's dress was beautiful as it was, but the style wasn't current. With a few changes, it honors Rebecca still. The local seamstress was able to update the dress to my specifications. I like that she removed the puffy mutton-leg sleeves and added bell sleeves instead. I was afraid she couldn't remove the heavy hoops and all those petticoats. I really wanted the dress to have a bustled skirt, and she worked a miracle. When I add the white kid-leather gloves and brocade one-inch heel shoes, my ensemble will be complete. I hope Allistair will be pleased with my appearance."

"He will be simply smitten because you are a vision of loveliness," Emma assured her.

"Speaking of loveliness," Victoria said, "that shade of pink on your gown is perfect for you. I wonder what your new husband will think. I've seen the way you look at each other. I guess the honeymoon stage isn't over. I'm so glad you are my matron of honor. I could not imagine anyone else in this role."

Emma blushed a darker pink color than her dress as she helped Victoria into her wedding gown. A knock on the door revealed it was Aunt Yolanda.

"My lovely niece, I have a special gift for you. The new wedding tradition is to give the bride something blue," she said, presenting Victoria with a snow-white handkerchief, beautifully embroidered in blue, with the bride and groom's initials plus the wedding date on it. "This will remind you that whenever you feel blue, just look at the handkerchief and remember you and Allistair are united and can face anything together.

"Victoria, I have good news to tell you. The young girl you helped escape from her abusive father has learned to read and write. She sent a letter to Whitehaven to thank them for helping her. She has a good job, in fact, and her son is growing so fast. She added a note for you. Her dad was arrested for killing his friend, Joe. She said neither of you has to worry about him anymore." Aunt Yolanda hugged Victoria before leaving.

Victoria looked around the new suite of rooms Lord John insisted she and Allistair make their own. It was at the end of the east wing because he thought they would need more privacy after they were married.

Hugging Emma, Victoria then walked toward Lord John, who stood waiting at the top of the stairs.

"Victoria, this brings back good memories. Your mother's wedding dress looks so beautiful on you. I love the changes you made. Allistair will be pleased when he sees you walk into the ballroom."

Victoria's heart leaped in her chest when the wedding march began, and they slowly walked down the stairs. Mother and Father Montgomery met them at the bottom, like angels at the pearly gates.

"Today is complete with you all being here to give me away," Victoria said, as Emma handed her a nosegay. Seeing the flowers in the bouquet was the first indication of how the ballroom was decorated. Martha wouldn't let Victoria or Allistair enter the room or see any of the decorations ahead of time.

The doors to the ballroom opened to a beautiful flower-filled wonderland, with the lovely strains of a harp greeting them.

She knew the symbolism of the flowers was

important. There were daisies for innocence, stephanotis for happiness in marriage, and orchids for true love. Martha arranged the flowers into huge bouquets and attached them to tall gold candlesticks. With white tulle draped between them, they served as lovely path markers on either side of the aisle. An archway covered with flowers and more tulle took a place of prominence at the far end of the aisle.

Emma swayed down the aisle, scattering rose petals. Victoria and her mother moved into view, followed by the two fathers. All four walked toward the archway where Allistair, his best man, Daniel, and an officiant stood.

Victoria only had eyes for Allistair. He looked so handsome in his white waistcoat and lavender doeskin trousers. He wore a black top hat and pearl-colored gloves with black embroidery.

The vows were a blur. Victoria remembered repeating the words the officiant said, especially "I do," but she could hardly wait for the pronouncement from him that she and Allistair were man and wife.

Everyone toasted the happy couple one more time as they feasted on the wedding cake. It was a fruitcake decorated with white frosting in ornate scrolled designs and topped with orange blossoms.

Afterward, Emma went with Victoria to help remove her wedding dress. A seductive nightgown from her mother was waiting for her.

"Victoria, since I just got married, do you want to talk about what to expect on your wedding night? Do you have any questions I can answer?" Emma asked, avoiding eye contact.

"Thanks, Emma, but I think I will wait for Allistair to help me with anything I don't understand. I'm sure everything will be wonderful," Victoria said with a secret smile remembering what Allistair had already taught her about love.

Minutes later, Victoria heard the door to their secluded suite open. She was standing at the window, looking at the full moon shining upon the lovely gardens below.

"Allistair, our wedding was perfect, and I know tonight will be also," said Victoria, glancing over her shoulder at Allistair, who slowly walked over and wrapped his arms around her.

He bent and lightly brushed his lips against one side of her neck, then switched to the other side. He turned her around, and he looked into her eyes before trailing a finger over her lips. The moonlight shown upon his face, and she clearly saw eternal bliss reflected in his cerulean eyes—the color of the sky where it embraced the sea's horizon. She trembled with anticipation as he slowly moved to kiss her, a kiss with such passion and love, he left her dazed with bliss.

"Victoria, your smile shines brighter than all the stars in the heavens." Slowly, Allistair removed her nightgown and looked upon her body with wonder in his eyes. He slowly reached out to touch her breasts, then his hand traced the curve of her hips. Victoria could only imagine the sensation of wrapping her legs around him as they made love.

He picked Victoria up and carried her to the bed. She wanted and hoped he would touch her as he had before.

Laying her gently down, Allistair settled beside her and began to manipulate both of her breasts with his thumbs, causing them to harden into tight buds. A small sigh escaped from her lips as she instinctively began to press herself against him. She bit her lower lip as he moved his hand from her breasts and pulled the pins from her hair. The blonde mass of curls cascading over the pillow seemed fascinating to him. A fascination that made Victoria realize a power over him she never knew a woman could have until now.

"Why have you stopped," she asked.

Allistair did not reply; instead, he moved his mouth to her left breast and ran his tongue leisurely over the bud. When he had his fill of one, he moved to the other as she squirmed from the exquisite torture.

"You are so beautiful. I love you and only want your pleasure," Allistair said, looking at her with transfixed eyes. Then, touching her silken thighs, he slowly moved toward her secret place. She thought she would die before he finally caressed her there and made her world awaken to pleasure that she had never imagined.

Victoria felt so full of love that she thought she would shatter. "Ooooh, Allistair, I feel like I will explode. I have never felt so alive and loved." She was glad they were the only ones with rooms located in the east wing of the manor.

Allistair quickly stood up and stepped back from the bed.

"Don't leave me," she cried.

"I'm not. Let me undress, and I'll join you again."

Allistair removed his shirt, revealing his broad, muscular chest. Victoria's eyes slowly followed the trail of dark hair as it disappeared beneath his trousers. Allistair watched to see her reaction as his drawers fell to the floor.

She had never seen a man completely unclothed. She could only stare at his pulsing shaft, his chiseled perfection.

He returned to the bed and covered her in kisses. He stroked her between her legs, and before long, he seemed to realize his hand was a violin bow that played every note of her quivering body. Victoria rubbed against him, shaking as wave after wave of ecstasy overwhelmed her senses. She was wet and ready for him.

"Victoria, this will hurt only the first time and only for a second; I will be as gentle as possible," he said, pulling her close. Then, unable to wait any longer, he shifted so he could slowly enter her. Victoria cried out once, but soon, she felt the sensations of pleasure.

She trembled uncontrollably as each movement brought her closer to her ultimate climax. Finally, Allistair reached between their bodies and stroked the spot that would send her over the moon. He arrived at the point of no return, groaning loudly with one last thrust. He seemed to find more pleasure studying her reaction.

Later, when they had recovered their breath, Allistair asked her to turn over. "Victoria, let me see the heart-shaped birthmark on your back near your right shoulder blade."

Kissing the birthmark was the start of another new and exciting way of making love.

"Oh, Allistair, you are a good teacher."

"And you, my darling, I will make sure you earn your masters in lovemaking."

They laughed as Allistair reached for her to teach her more.

He was right; Victoria realized their wedding night did include fireworks. Allistair had kept his promise, and together they explored each other's bodies, discovering such pleasure.

Chapter Thirty~Seven: The Future is Bright

TWO YEARS passed with boundless joy and deep sadness as life goes. Martha was the first to realize Victoria was pregnant.

"Victoria, have you been sick the last few mornings before breakfast?" Martha asked, after Victoria almost ran from the breakfast room for the third time in a row. "I have noticed you turn green whenever the men talk about new foals being born. They are descriptive with their stories even at the breakfast table since most foals are delivered overnight. Dear, do you think you could be with child? I remember when I was pregnant with Allistair, I had morning sickness for a month."

"Martha, I think I am." Victoria had to sit down. "What will I do? I'm frightened. What if something goes wrong?"

"Everything will be fine. I will introduce you to the

island midwife, Helga Koppers, who has twenty years of experience delivering babies. Her mother was the island midwife for thirty years before her. She even delivered Allistair twenty-six years ago. Helga was her apprentice then. She can also give you advice on nutrition before and after delivery. She has helped many women on the island who had trouble breastfeeding. I trust her completely.

"We'll also have Dr. Williams examine you. He will be present at the birth." Martha did a little dance. "I'm going to be a grandmother."

After an examination by both Helga and Dr. Williams, Victoria was excited to tell Allistair. "Sweetie, I have great news. We are having a baby."

"Victoria, are you sure?" Allistair asked, the color draining from his face.

"Yes, my love. Dr. Williams and the island midwife confirmed I am pregnant."

"I've never held a newborn before. What if I drop him?"

"You will be a wonderful Father. So, you think we are having a boy? Well, I have a feeling it's going to be a girl. I guess we will have to wait and see," said Victoria.

To know she carried new life made Victoria cry tears of joy. Allistair couldn't help but grin from ear and ear.

Her mother, Aunt Yolanda, and other women on the island gave her instructions to follow before her "lying-in" period started. Some older ladies even offered to concoct her potions for morning sickness.

"Victoria, remember that the amount of morning sickness a mother-to-be has will determine the gender. If you are sick a lot, then you are having a girl. If you only feel queasy a little bit, then you are having a boy." Mother wrote when she heard the good news that she would be a grandmother.

Aunt Yolanda wrote that craving sour, salty, or spicy foods mean that a baby boy is on the way. If you crave sweets or dairy, then you are having a girl.

Allistair seemed to suffer some of the same physical symptoms as Victoria, such as nausea, heartburn, abdominal pain, and backaches.

Daniel patted Allistair on the stomach and said, "When is it due?"

"Your time is coming. Laura will become pregnant, then I will remind you of this," Allistair said to Daniel.

The first time Victoria felt the movement of the baby was around five months.

"Mrs. Victoria, you are having twins," Dr. Williams was pleased to tell her.

"How will I tell Allistair? I think you should be present in case he faints," Victoria laughed.

Knowing now that she was carrying twins, the midwife, along with Dr. Williams, made plans to attend the birth.

One room near Victoria's suite had been prepared as a birthing room in anticipation of the arrival of the twins. Helga had consulted on what was needed in the room to ensure a safe delivery.

Both the Montgomerys and the Stanfords made plans to come to the island the week the twins were due. Daniel and Laura were also coming back to Swan Island at the same time.

Three weeks before Victoria was due to give birth, the first hint that she was in labor was when a backache started to irritate her early in the morning. By noon, the backache had gone from faint to severe. Martha had informed her that twins could come early.

"Ooooh, Allistair, I'm in labor. Please have someone get Helga and Dr. Williams." Victoria tried to stay calm, but she couldn't mask the fear in her voice.

Victoria panted and whimpered involuntarily as Allistair closed the door to the birthing room. The cramping pain increased, leaving Victoria gasping for breath. Each contraction felt as if her insides were slowly twisting tighter and tighter until it was almost unbearable, and then the pain would subside. She found if she mentally accepted the pain, the birthing process would be more bearable. Not pain-free but bearable.

Martha helped supply hot water, towels, and held Victoria's hand.

Allistair remembered being excited when Victoria told him she was with child. A couple of months later, when she said they were having twins, he was delighted but also afraid. What if something happened to Victoria or the twins?

"Allistair, four feet keep kicking me in the ribs. Here, feel," she said, but every time he tried to feel them kicking at the same time, they wouldn't. They only kicked together when Victoria was alone.

Three weeks early? The babies are coming three weeks early? Allistair panicked upon hearing the news.

Victoria told him it was time to get the doctor and the midwife. He ran down the stairs, yelling for Daniel, who was in the parlor.

"Hurry! Find Dr. Williams—and the midwife. Victoria is in labor."

Allistair sprinted back up the stairs, almost running over his mother as she entered Victoria's rooms.

"Son, help Victoria move into the birthing room. Then you can either go to your rooms or down to the parlor. Sorry, but men aren't allowed to stay for the birth."

"I love you, my darling." Allistair kissed Victoria.

"You have to go now," Martha said. "I will let you know when the babies are born."

Who made the rule that men couldn't be in the birthing room? Allistair wondered. He wanted to be there should his wife need him.

Victoria let loose a blood-curdling scream, which came through the closed door. No, men shouldn't be in the birthing room. His knees buckled and sweat broke out on the back of his neck before he rushed to tell Lord John the babies were coming.

"I'm glad Lord John's rooms are in the other wing of the manor. Hearing Victoria scream would have upset him. I thought I would stay in our suite of rooms, but I think waiting with you in the parlor is best," he said to Daniel, after Dr. Williams and Helga hurried upstairs to Victoria.

Allistair and Victoria were overjoyed to welcome the twins to the DuPree family. She was in labor for sixteen hours before baby Rebecca Esther made her appearance. Allistair John was born twenty minutes later.

"Allistair and Daniel, come see the babies," Martha called down to them from the second-story landing.

She met them outside the birthing-room door where she presented baby girl, Becky, and the midwife presented baby boy, A.J., to their father first. Allistair kissed them then entered to check on Victoria.

"Darling, you have done an excellent job bringing our babies into this world. I know you are exhausted, but you positively glow and have never looked more beautiful to me since the day I met you."

"Martha, you are the perfect grandmother. Thank you for babysitting. Becky and A.J. love playing with you. Allistair

261

and I don't care if you spoil them. That's what grandmothers should do," Victoria said.

Martha gave Allistair and Victoria plenty of alone time. The twins seemed to help her regain her happiness. In addition, Martha was "talking" to Emma's father, Simon. That's what she called her romance with him.

The Montgomerys and Stanfords visited as often as possible. Allistair and Victoria traveled to London to see them when the twins were one year old.

Victoria was happy that Laura would soon be her sister-in-law. She helped with the wedding plans and agreed to be her matron of honor. One night, close to the wedding day, Daniel asked Victoria to stay and talk with him as everyone else left the parlor.

"Laura and I will live on Swan Island with Sir Samuel," Daniel informed her. "We will only be ten minutes away, and we can send messages by carrier pigeon any time you start to miss me." Daniel tried to laugh but got choked up. "I love you, sister, and I'm glad you came home."

Father was Daniel's best man. Victoria was blessed to see the pride on both of their faces. She knew Daniel was glad Father was still with them and able to be at his wedding.

Emma helped Victoria find another lady's maid to take her place. "Emma found Sue for me," Victoria said to Allistair. "She wouldn't turn over the duties to someone who couldn't meet her high standards, so I know I have the best person. I understand why she had to relinquish her job with me. Having a toddler and another baby on the way takes up a lot of time. Emma and Steve's baby boy is so cute. He's learning to walk and will be everywhere soon. I'm glad our babies have one playmate with another on the way."

Grandmother Esther lived for another year, and Victoria's heart had overflowed with joy to see her and Lord John grow so close again. That year, Victoria and Esther continued their talks in the gardens but during the day instead of at night. Victoria would miss their conversations so much.

The twins brought Father immeasurable joy. Sadly, he peacefully passed away six months after their first birthday. Father was buried in the island cemetery next to Rebecca's grave.

"Now that I have inherited the Barony," said Daniel, "Laura and I will need to split our time between Swan Island and the townhouse in London. You and Allistair will have to come during the London Season and stay with us."

Victoria couldn't help counting her blessings while Allistair sat on the nursery floor, laughing at Becky and A.J., who were trying to crawl.

"Allistair, I need to tell you something," she said, caressing her stomach. "We will have a third baby in about six months."

"Wow." Allistair jumped to his feet and grabbed Victoria before dancing with her around the nursery. The twins clapped and laughed as their eyes followed their parents, who swirled across the floor, trying to avoid stepping on the children's toys.

Victoria reminisced about her twenty-first birthday. She never dreamed she would know such joy. The journey to her "happily ever after" began that morning years ago when she learned she had been left on a doorstep.

THE END

About the Author

By the time Beatrice was eighteen, she practically lived at her local library. Her favorite genres were Romantic Suspense, Mystery, and Thrillers — particularly those set in England. After graduating from high school, she wrote pages and pages of a story that she was sure would soon be published and make her rich. Then life took her in a different direction, and her writing shifted from fiction to business books, where she won three national awards through the American Advertising Federation. Beatrice came across her manuscript last year, and the story called to her, saying NOW is the time. Trying to read her teenage pencil scratches on old notebook pages wasn't easy, but the story, Left on a Doorstep, was still in her.

Beatrice also writes poetry, usually as a subject comes to her. As a positive person, most of the poems are uplifting and come from a place of compassion and deep emotion.

Beatrice lives with her husband of 31 years, Milan Sergent, who is a multi-award-winning author.

To learn more about her works, visit www.beatricecrew.com. While there, join her mailing list for important news updates and notifications about future novel releases.

https://www.facebook.com/BeatriceH.Crew
https://mobile.twitter.com/BeatriceHCrew